"My goal," Gisele said softly, *"is to tame you."*

If Edward had possessed the energy, he would have physically struck out at her. "Tame? As a master would tame a wild animal?"

"You are not wild, merely...misunderstood."

"You should have listened to your pal Sam," Edward said, working at his chains, hating the fact that he could not fight back, or even fight at all. "He had sense enough to know that I will not take to any taming."

Gisele paused, got a speculative twinkle in her eyes, then slowly lowered herself to all fours, crawling toward him until she was in his line of sight. Her erotic pose caused lust to surge through him, his gaze sheering to a brutal red tinge that colored her every move.

He was turned on, almost out of control.

"You know," she said, "the more you resist, the more you challenge me." She bit her lip softly, driving him crazy with desire.

"And I do adore a good challenge, Edward."

Blaze™

Dear Reader,

When my editor read the end of *The Ultimate Bite* (July 2007), she asked if Edward, the "rogue vampire," was going to have his own story. Since I'd been hoping she'd wonder about that, I answered an unqualified yes!

After all, Edward genuinely wanted to redeem himself; he'd just gone about it in a mercenary way. And at the end of the book, when the vampire Gisele robbed him of the one thing he believed would redeem him—turning human again—he seemed to be on the edge of a big journey, one that included giving Gisele some payback, of course.

And that brings us to the beginning of this story. I think you'll see that Edward and Gisele have a lot to teach each other. Naturally, they do it in a very Blaze-like fashion, but that's what made this book so much fun to write!

Enjoy,

Crystal Green
www.crystal-green.com

GOOD TO THE LAST BITE
Crystal Green

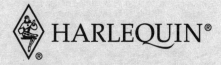

HARLEQUIN®

TORONTO • NEW YORK • LONDON
AMSTERDAM • PARIS • SYDNEY • HAMBURG
STOCKHOLM • ATHENS • TOKYO • MILAN • MADRID
PRAGUE • WARSAW • BUDAPEST • AUCKLAND

ISBN-13: 978-0-373-79430-0
ISBN-10:   0-373-79430-4

GOOD TO THE LAST BITE

Copyright © 2008 by Chris Marie Green.

www.eHarlequin.com

Printed in U.S.A.

ABOUT THE AUTHOR

Crystal Green lives near Las Vegas, Nevada, where she writes for the Harlequin Blaze and Silhouette Special Edition lines as well as penning vampire tales. She loves to read, overanalyze movies, practice yoga, travel and detail her obsessions on her Web page, www.crystal-green.com. She particularly enjoyed the Kentucky setting for this book, since she spent a few years in Danville during her wild (hah!) youth.

Books by Crystal Green

HARLEQUIN BLAZE

121—PLAYMATES
179—BORN TO BE BAD
261—INNUENDO
303—JINXED!
    "Tall, Dark & Temporary"
334—THE ULTIMATE BITE
387—ONE FOR THE ROAD

SILHOUETTE SPECIAL EDITION

1574—HER MONTANA
    MILLIONAIRE
1587—THE BLACK SHEEP HEIR
1668—THE MILLIONAIRE'S
    SECRET BABY
1670—A TYCOON IN TEXAS
1724—PAST IMPERFECT
1752—THE LAST COWBOY
1838—THE PLAYBOY
    TAKES A WIFE

Don't miss any of our special offers. Write to us at the following address for information on our newest releases.

Harlequin Reader Service
U.S.: 3010 Walden Ave., P.O. Box 1325, Buffalo, NY 14269
Canadian: P.O. Box 609, Fort Erie, Ont. L2A 5X3

To Brenda Chin, my awesome editor,
who suggested that Edward carry on
with his own story!

1

GISELE was hungry tonight.

As she sat on one side of the hotel atrium's rectangular bar, the appetite gnawed at her from the inside out—burning through her with a destructive ache that tightened her belly. She had not taken sustenance for a couple of days, so it was time to feast.

Her keen gaze traveled the bar area, indoor foliage masking rain-spattered, summer-night-shaded windows and hovering over businessmen who had undone their ties as they nursed that one last beer before bedtime. She could detect slight tan lines on ring fingers, could infer the restless longing for company on a sales trip.

Gisele did not even need to reach into their minds to know their stories. The tale was always the same from bar to bar, city to city, state to state.

And it only made hunting for a meal that much easier.

Now her focus rested on one man in particular, a broad-shouldered stud in a pinstriped button-down who had already smiled at her for too long, his interest predatory.

She smiled back, taking care not to show her teeth so he would have no idea what he was inviting.

Her pulse hammered, her canines pushing at her gums in anticipation of tonight's drink—the blood she needed, the satiation it would bring.

She waited for the businessman to come to her and, sure enough, he snatched his beer bottle from the bar's surface and made his way around the corner, aiming for the open stool next to hers.

"You look pretty lonely," he said, his voice sales-call smooth, his bluegrass cadence telling her that he was local, maybe even from here in Lexington.

She lifted a brow, encouraging him, laying out her trap.

Then, out of the corner of her gaze, she saw Sam, her twentyish-looking vampire comrade, sidling closer to the businessman's back. Her partner blended into the crowd, his sandy hair spiky, his lanky body in L.L. Bean-catalogue clothing while he listened to an iPod. He looked like a fraternity boy from the nearby University of Kentucky out for a late-night drink.

But Gisele had also caught something else in her peripheral vision. A flicker.

A scorching feeling, really.

A sense of being watched and noticed?

She glanced around, but found nothing amiss. Perhaps she was only reacting to the attention men paid to her appearance; after all, she had chosen to wear her tightest, most provocative red dress, and it clung to her body—that of an eternal twenty-two-year-old's—like an exotic oil slathered over skin.

Even so, she remained alert, her flesh alive with a strange heat she had never experienced in all her thirty-plus years of being a vampire….

During her pause, the businessman had backed off slightly. "Hey, just let me know if I'm invading your space. I only thought you might like someone to buy you a drink."

She turned her full attention on him. "I *would* like. How about an amaretto over ice?"

His eyes lit up at her barely there French inflection; she had spent so many recent years in America that her accent—and many human instincts—had settled to a hint by now.

The dreamy young human girl fresh from university, the wonderer who had sought meaning from movies because she was not getting it from life, was only a bare memory.

Within seconds, the businessman had summoned the bartender, put a twenty-dollar bill on the bar and ordered her a beverage that she did not intend to imbibe. She was never thirsty for anything but blood, yet pretending she drank normally was a part of survival.

All the while, Sam inched closer to the businessman. Gisele knew her partner well enough to realize he had noted where their mark had stowed his wallet in his pants pocket.

Sam's human life as a pickpocket on the streets of late nineteenth-century New York came in very handy.

"So where're you from?" the businessman asked.

She negligently flicked her wrist. "Here. There."

"Ah. A cryptic woman."

"No. I am just not much for settling down."

For good reason, she thought, as the businessman took a swig of his beer, gave her a lingering scan and drummed his fingers on the bar. During the last two years, she and Sam had moved quickly and frequently, surviving in their own way, fugitives from yet another vampire—one she had created in the aftermath of a crisis.

Edward.

While she tasted the memory of his blood on her tongue, his image clouded her mind, just as it did so often. With his dark-brown hair worn long to his jaw, he reminded her of the actor Johnny Depp playing the part of a rakish highwayman. The stirring impression was only emphasized by sloping cheekbones and a lithe, dangerous way of moving.

But his amber eyes always cut into the romance of the fantasy because they were so intense with the hatred she had earned when she had robbed him of the humanity he had so desperately sought....

The impulsive half of Gisele yearned for her created to find her, to be near. Yet, a disillusioned creature, Edward would not come in peace. After all, he had been in search of a soul, haunted by centuries of emptiness. And knowing that the only way for his kind to get his humanity back was to kill his creator, Edward had hunted down his estranged maker, drawing Fegan out of the shadows by draining blood from human women in Fegan's territory. Ultimately, Edward had murdered his master, reclaiming his soul and reaching his dream of becoming human again.

But as her revenge for him beheading the beloved mentor who had adopted Gisele when she had been but a new, confused vampire, herself, she had turned Edward *back* into a so-called monster.

Afterward, she had flown from him in an act of self-preservation, thinking that his old friends, the rest of Fegan's vampire set, also turned human, might gather weapons and slay her for what she had done to Edward.

The thing was, ever since biting him, he had become a part of her, an extension of her own self, and she could not forget how he had made her crave more of his blood, his presence.

Even though they had never had sex, which could heighten the sensation of a bite, there had never been a taste like Edward's.

Oddly enough, she did not feel that way about her other created, Sam. She never had to chase away an ever-present ache for him.

So why did she long for another taste of the vampire who hated her? And why was the craving like nothing she had ever experienced before?

Warped, that was what she was, because, if Edward ever caught her, she had no doubt he would exact vengeance. Besides, Gisele was now the only thing standing between him and his soul.

As the businessman nattered on, the bartender delivered her beverage, and she cupped the glass in her hands, condensation making her palms wet. Why hadn't she just left well enough alone when Edward had murdered Fegan? Why had she bitten and then turned him again?

Why even ask? Fegan, her surrogate father, had meant everything to her.

Yet, now that time had passed, she sometimes thought about finding Edward, herself, just so she might palaver with him—to seek an understanding or, if it came down to it, to tame him into an acceptance of their new bond. Taming him would be a matter of survival, since it would not do to have a vampire running around intent upon ending her existence.

She brushed off something that a human might define as remorse. It was not so much an emotion as an acknowledgment that she had brought more trouble upon herself by recklessly exchanging with Edward.

"So you're one of those free spirits." The businessman clearly had no idea that she had tuned out of the one-sided conversation for a while.

"Yes." Back in the seventies, as a human, she had been into free love, having her share of men with no attachment to any of them. The trend continued even now, although she would not call her physical expressions "love."

"I've always liked that kind of woman," he added. "I could tell right away that you're a little different from most gals I see on my road trips."

He was no doubt inviting her to ask about his profession, but Gisele had been through so many hunts that this leg of the activity bored her. She knew what he wanted, and the quicker he believed he would get it, the better.

Bluntly, she slid a hand onto his leg near his pocket. He sucked in a breath, and she knew it was not only because he could feel the coolness of her fingers through his trousers.

While he was distracted by her touch, Sam deftly moved in closer, slid out the man's wallet, then left the bar, going back to his room until they could meet up again.

After she had fed.

"How would your wife feel about this?" Gisele asked, squeezing his thigh for emphasis.

The businessman's skin grew ruddy. "I…"

Gisele tilted her head, considering him. "No need to explain. You have an unhappy marriage. I understand."

She tightened her grip ever so slightly, then slid her palm down until she came to the middle of his thigh. There, she inserted her fingers between his legs.

He fumbled his beer onto the bar, spilling it.

Then she felt it again….

Zzzzzzmmmm—

That same rattling-hot sensation of being watched too hard, too intensely.

A shiver—an erotic thrill—consumed her, and she glanced around the bar, scanning for a source of the electric invasion. But she did not see anyone's gaze on her.

Then all traces of the zinging discomfort were gone. Just like that.

Gathering her composure, she leaned closer to the businessman. His blood pumped wildly, and she absorbed every throb through her fingers, through the air and into her skin.

So hungry….

"Just wondering," she whispered. "Is this how you improve your marital relations? By honing your libido on the road so you can favor your wife with your new expertise?"

The businessman swallowed, and there was guilt in his gaze. Yet, just as Gisele gained some hope for him, his eyes went hazy with desire again.

She might have sought out someone else for the night if he had changed his mind.

The music of his heartbeat pummeled her ears and danced in her belly, escalating her taut appetite.

Putting on a saucy grin, she slid off her stool, her fingers trailing out from between his knees.

If he was not going to back out, then she would go forward.

"Lighten up," she said. "I am only giving you grief. Married, engaged…I do not mind."

Then she crooked a finger at him, backing away toward the bar's exit.

He followed, just as she knew he would.

Now the rest of the routine: get him to her room, soothe this willing victim with her voice and mind, take her fill of him, then stop the flow of blood from his wound with the psychic fusion of her touch, leaving crusted punctures that would heal rapidly. Her bite wouldn't cause him to become a vampire—he would also have to drink her blood for that—and a caress to the temple would cloud the details of the interaction, providing her a measure of secrecy.

Fegan had often laughed at her insistence on "fixing up" their victims after a bite, calling her—and the rest of his family—"vampires with soul." But none of them had been as old as Fegan, or as in need of as much stimulation to alleviate the unending passage of days....

Forgetting Fegan in her growing hunger, she led her victim through the hotel lobby, knowing that tomorrow night, she and Sam would repeat a similar process for his sake. Sam had taken his own meal earlier, but the newer vampire required more frequent feedings. Gisele, herself, would not need to hunt again for a few more nights—not unless *she* required some stimulation.

She turned the corner into the first-floor hallway where she had a room. Her body was pounding, her veins growling in famished greed.

She glanced over her shoulder to offer encourage-ment to her prey, but before she could open her mouth, a room door opened and she was bowled over by the same jolting awareness she had sensed back in the bar—

The rattle of silver was the only sound she heard as a chain wrapped around her bare shoulders, her arms, drag-ging her into the dim room. The door eased shut before the businessman even came around the corner.

The silver sapped energy from her skin—from her *core*—and she fell against a wall, sliding down as her fingers grasped for purchase.

Vaguely, she heard the businessman's voice outside as he called for her, but she could not answer. She did not have the strength.

Silver...the weakness of every vampire she knew....

"Hello, Gisele," her captor said from behind her, a schooled British accent dancing over her skin with its refined edge, then plunging into her and leaving her gasping.

Her senses filled with a scent—a remembered taste—that had haunted her for two years.

Gisele turned to see who it was, even though she already knew.

Edward, looming like a tall avenger in a bulky Second-World-War-style military coat and gloved hands that were holding her chain as if it were a leash. His mouth tilted in a cruel smile—a gentleman hunter who had caught his prey—and his eyes blazed with fury, his high cheekbones lending him a triumphant arrogance.

Finally caught, she thought as her body dissolved into an instinctive need that split her from sex to chest, leaving her open to him.

More vulnerable than she had ever been, even in life.

JUST KILL her now, Edward thought. *Take the stake from your bag and drive it through her heart so you can be human again.*

Before his fateful encounter with Gisele, that was all he'd wanted for nearly three centuries of existence—a return to humanity. And he'd even possessed it when he had exterminated Fegan from the face of the earth. With the death of his first creator, Edward had been blissfully mortal for moments, drinking in the profound beauty of a soul returned.

Then Gisele had taken it all away by re-turning him.

Unfortunately, she had never understood Fegan's evil, had never even recognized it. Or maybe she had, and that was just one more reason she deserved extermination, too. It was the only way Edward knew of to regain his own humanity—kill the one who had savagely made him this way for the second time in his existence.

Now, he took in the sight of her slouching down the hotel room's wall. It was satisfying to see her so weakened by the silver, from which his gloves were protecting him.

He cocked his head. At the moment, Gisele wasn't his worst nightmare so much as a slumped woman in a sinful red dress, her black hair worn to the shoulders in a modern cut, her brown eyes the color of dying suns. Her body was sleek and long, yet still somehow demure as she plopped the rest of the way to the carpet.

A thrust of…something…speared him. At first, he'd dreamed of avenging himself on her, detailing how he would capture her, how he would put her through as much agony as she'd put him through, how he would finish her off. But month by month, the fantasies had turned more…carnal.

He'd found himself opening to thoughts of her mouth, sucking, kissing, melting his body with a white heat that left him nearly breathless.

Yet, always, he would stop the dream from continuing. Then all that would remain was the anger, because there was no room inside him for anything *but* revenge.

"So, the night has come," he said, his voice ragged. "Sam left you alone, and here we are, together again. I can't think of a lovelier scenario."

"You plan to kill me now?" she asked, her words barely threaded together with exhaustion.

But she didn't sound afraid. Not Gisele.

"My dear," he said, fisting the chain, "*killing* is such a common word for what I'm about to do. The phrase *extending poetic karma* seems far more appropriate."

So do it, he thought.

Nevertheless, he found himself hesitating.

How could that be? He—the rogue vampire who had so singlemindedly gone after his own creator. Had two years of listening to his friends' pleas affected him? Had he been swayed by all the arguments to desist given by his former vampire family, who had also become human when Fegan had expired?

Roger, Rupert, Henry and, most importantly, Stephen, who had found love and peace with a human woman— they had *all* told Edward that he would never find a state of grace through murdering Gisele. And, somewhere deep down, he knew they were right. Yet how else would he reclaim his soul if not through her death?

Gisele was watching him with those startling eyes, and his cock twitched. The sensation was so forceful that he tightened his gloved grip on the chains. Centuries ago—that was the last time his body had been stimulated this powerfully….

He blocked her from entering his mind, from taking him over from the inside out.

"Lucky you bound me with silver first," she finally whispered, leaning her head back against the wall, her breath starting to even out. "As a new vampire, you are not strong enough to best me without help, are you? Out of these chains, I would overcome you before you could even take another breath."

Too true. As a re-turned vampire, he'd gone back to square one, his strength, speed and skills weaker than an older vampire's. He could only gain power with time, even though his brain already knew precisely what his body could do if it only had the abilities it had lost upon becoming temporarily mortal.

When Gisele exchanged blood with him, he had essentially been reborn into this existence he had despised for so long.

Deliberately, he moved closer to his nemesis, glared at her then wrapped the rest of the chains around her torso so he could be assured that they wouldn't be easily thrust off.

He tried not to look at her breasts, her body, even though the effort sapped him.

Fortunately, she didn't resist. She couldn't.

In the end, Edward stepped back, surveying his handiwork. But then Gisele's eyes met his, and a craving flared through him before he could look away.

How? He hated her with every cell of his being.

But that didn't explain all those idle, presleep moments when her graceful body, her very scent had been an opiate to him. When he'd dreamed of a contentment he'd never found in any of his incarnations.

Of course, he would always catch himself and banish the notion, leaving his senses utterly scrambled.

Perhaps it was only his passion for vengeance that twisted her through his fantasies. His mind playing games, mistaking sexual lust for what he truly wanted—justice.

He moved toward the duffel bag on the bed. "I seem to have caught you before you ruined another unsuspecting male tonight. From what I saw, you and Sam have quite the set-up, picking a mark's pockets and then moving on to what he carries in his veins."

"Long ago," Gisele rasped, "you did the same, centuries before I joined the gang."

"I didn't know any better back then."

It was true that after having been turned out of hearth and home by his mother's brother after her long-in-coming death, Edward had found himself desperate enough to pluck a coin or two out of pockets at the public houses. His work in the stables had not helped him cover the debts he'd incurred from caring for his sick mother, so, like the bastard he'd been born, he'd resorted to thievery.

Then one night, Fegan had caught him, persuaded him that he had all the answers, and then recruited Edward into the vampire gang.

Highwaymen, they'd been called before Edward had seen too much of the world to continue living in such depravity.

Reaching into the bag, he felt the rough surface of a stake, even through his thick glove. "Unlike the rest of Fegan's gang, Gisele, you do not seem to have learned any lessons."

A faint, harsh laugh. "I suppose I have not."

He thought about how his anger—his passion for justice, he told himself—had only grown while stalking her these past couple of years. How it had come to a peak when he had finally tracked her here to Lexington where she had cornered that businessman tonight. By the time she had touched her prey's thigh, Edward's rage had gotten to the point where he had forced himself to glance away, lest he explode.

He extracted the stake from the bag and faced her. The weapon gleamed in the low light, its sharp shadow cast over the wall. "I'd heard rumors, but I saw with my own eyes how you corrupted Sam again."

The chains clanked as she angled toward him. "He loved this life, Edward, and felt no gratitude to you for freeing him from it. The night I exchanged with you, Sam found me outside the hideout while I was still reeling from Fegan's murder. He begged me to return him to what he was before."

"So you took pity on him and performed the exchange."

"I only gave him what he wanted."

"Very touching. How ever did you find a heart in that hollow chest of yours?"

She paused. "A heart. I do not have much use for one of those nowadays."

"Why, Gisele… This news…it would *shock* even the most callous of beings."

Smiling slightly at his sarcasm, she said, "Believe it or not, turning you did not sit well with me." She closed her eyes, as if very tired. "Fegan was gone—my guiding force for so many years when everyone else in life had disappointed me. *Gone.* I did not mean to attack you— it was merely a reaction to *your* savagery."

A tight smile was his only response to that.

"Truly." Gisele sighed and opened her eyes. "All I wished to do was take what meant the most to you, just as you had taken what meant the most to me."

You should have killed me instead, he thought.

He held the stake by his side and took satisfaction from how Gisele's gaze lingered on the weapon. But she didn't seem afraid, only…resigned.

He had left Fegan's gang well before they had adopted Gisele, so he didn't know her, save for what Stephen and the rest of the gang had recently told him. But by all accounts, she could be wicked.

He didn't buy the resigned act for even a moment.

Yet there was something inside him that gnarled and bent until it pained, and it ratcheted up Edward's smoldering rage.

What was it? *Why* was it even there?

He moved toward her, and the closer he got, the more his skin hummed. Was it because he was already savoring this moment: the prospect of finally recovering what had always eluded him, the miracles that a soul could bring?

Or was it because of the way her dress draped to midthigh, revealing pale, tender skin?

His groin tightened, beating with a need that tossed him off-balance. He fortified himself, inspecting the stake in the light, taunting her. "Why is it that I have despised all of my creators? My good-for-nothing human father—the duke who seduced a chambermaid—who would ultimately not claim me. Fegan the monster. *You.* Do you suppose I have authority issues, Gisele?"

"Why toy with me?" She was watching him with a lowered gaze, giving the impression that she was fully in control. "You can run me through now, so do it."

"You'll have to beg more than that, dear."

Gisele stared straight ahead, as if bored. Then, once again, she smiled slightly, as if coming upon a fine idea. She languidly stretched as much as she could under the chains.

Edward couldn't help following the sultry length of her with his gaze.

"Edward," she whispered, a trace of vocal sway lining her tone.

But he was so shielded against her weakened efforts that her vampire tricks had no effect.

He bent to his haunches, testing her like the devil he was. "You have no fear, do you?"

"Why should I?"

For a moment, he wondered if she was stronger than these silver chains, and was merely entertaining herself by fooling him with this show of weakness. Yet that was unlikely. Only a much older, more powerful vampire than Gisele might be able to overcome the bindings.

He leaned closer to her, still toying. "Most would think it unwise for you to push a man in my position."

"I am only wondering why you have not struck fast and…hard." She licked the corner of her mouth, then scanned him, as if starving. "Do not forget that I spent years hearing the boys talk about 'the good days' with you during the few occasions Fegan was off hunting on his own. I also know you were the rogue vampire who drained several women to near-death in Las Vegas simply to get Fegan's attention, to draw him out. Such a ruthless man would not hesitate with me tonight."

Edward throttled the stake.

Use it.

But his friends' voices kept hounding him. *How can murder truly cleanse you? Humanity is in how you act, even if you are a vampire.*

A furious tremble clenched his stomach. He had her at his mercy, and his soul was literally seconds away from returning to him. But his old gang had planted a seed of doubt that kept growing, overcoming him now.

Even if he had remained human after exterminating Fegan, would he have been absolutely freed from darkness? Or would the act of killing still have weighed him down, just as if he had no soul at all?

He realized he was thinking about this too much, as usual.

That he was too distracted by the smooth flesh peeking out of that red dress.

Do it.

Gisele's breathing had quickened, as if his proximity

had an effect on her. Out of pure cruelty, he tested if this were true, leaning nearer, face-to-face.

She parted her lips, breathless now, and a surge of power lit through him, exciting him.

"You get off on danger, do you?" he asked. "Have you become so desensitized to everything else?"

"Perhaps I have."

At the purr of her voice, his blood pounded, calling up all his taboo fantasies. The taste of her—after that night it had grown, dogged him....

Maybe she read his expression—his bad fantasies painting themselves over his gaze, his mouth.

"I could give you such pleasure," she said softly. "I could erase all your romantic thoughts about becoming human again. You see what they do to themselves: the wars, the rotting of their societies. If you were human, you would only be more disillusioned."

"If I were fortunate enough to become human—" he began.

But she wasn't finished. "You do not see what you have. I doubt you ever did. The grass is always greener on the other side for Edward Marburn—"

He cut off her words by gripping her thigh, but at the contact, a thrill seared him. Sexual and devastating.

Seeing his response, she smiled, slowly parting her legs and biting her bottom lip.

A vampire, he kept telling himself. A creature who was playing a luring game, just as they all did. Gisele was attempting to distract him so she could buy time, go free.

"You want to have me as much as you want to kill me," she whispered. "I prefer the first option."

He tried not to picture how wet she might be, how slick her folds would feel if he discarded a glove and worked her with his fingers. It had been such a long time since he had enjoyed a woman, human or vampire....

The stake felt like the world's weight in his hand, but he couldn't bring himself to lift it. He couldn't bring himself to take her up on her offer, either, even though the urge to do so was overwhelming.

But she didn't seem to notice his indecision. No, her head was cocked, as if she were attuned to a distant sound.

And, too late, he heard it: the running footsteps, the door flying open under another vampire's strength.

Before Edward could even raise the stake and plunge it into Gisele, Sam, his former gang member, had crashed into him, driving him away from her.

She must have been calling to him, even faintly, with her mind....

Automatically, Edward's fangs protruded, his back hunched as he got to all fours and prepared to pounce on Sam. But the other vampire had already whipped the comforter off the bed and used it to remove Gisele's chains.

Her restored speed and strength made it no contest from that point on.

As Edward sprang, she used the bedspread to pick up the chains, then she stepped out of his path and wrapped the restraints around Edward's bare neck while bringing him in a controlled arc to the floor.

Because of the silver, the energy seeped out of him, and he could only stare at her from the carpet.

So close. He had almost had her.

But he would not give up this fight. It was only beginning.

He flashed fang at her. "Time for you to do away with me, mademoiselle?"

Gisele watched him in disbelief—and perhaps some

amusement—as Sam took up her back, silent and clearly furious.

"I am not letting you off so easily," she said. "Now that you've found me, I am not about to let *you* go."

2

"I CAN'T believe you," Sam said as he and Gisele sat in the dark at the kitchen table in the abandoned home they had discovered just outside Lexington a few nights ago. Behind him, a window showcased moon-shaded fields of tumbling green hills laced together by white fences and oak trees. "You've gone insane, chaining up that mad thing and bringing him back here with us."

Sam was the only creature who could talk to her in that manner and get away with it.

Back when she had been adopted into the gang—the lone female among all the boys—Sam had become as much of a brother to her as Fegan had been a father figure. They were the pseudo-family she had sorely needed in a time of great confusion: she had been newly turned and abandoned by her mysterious creator, and her feral ways had even prompted her own parents to kick her out of their dingy apartment in the 10th arrondissement of Paris.

She had seen that coming for months though.

After graduating through a hard-won scholarship from university, she had been living at home while saving her money to pursue a higher degree in visual arts. Days, she had served in a café and then gone on to her night job selling tickets at the cinema, where she would always sneak to the seats once the film had started. But after the change, when Gisele's mother had caught her sucking the blood out of a slab of raw meat because she was afraid to give in to her base instincts and drink from an actual person, her parents had forced her out.

Gisele had never returned. How could she when she'd had no idea what precisely had happened to her after the seductive bite and consequent blood exchange with the dark stranger?

Bewildered, she had wandered the streets, not knowing what to do or how to appease this new hunger that had taken hold of her. Fortunately, after a few nights spent huddling in dark corners and stealing blood from passed-out drunks, she had found Fegan and the gang outside the door of a tourist-laden cabaret nightclub, where they were busy picking pockets. She had sensed that they were somehow like her and had slyly helped in their petty crimes, coming back the next night, too, insinuating herself into Fegan's affections bit by bit and educating herself in all their criminal tricks. They'd quickly realized that her feminine wiles made her a valuable asset, allowing the gang to go after bigger scores: rich men who were more focused on seductive Gisele than their priceless art or their vaults.

In exchange, Fegan had taught her what it was to be a vampire—something her own elusive creator had not bothered to do for some reason.

"Sam," she said affectionately now, "you forget that I am much stronger than you or Edward these days. We confiscated the weapons in his slayer bag, so he has no way of terminating me—especially not from where he is right this minute."

Which was up in the attic, chained to the wall with the same silver he had used to bind her back at the hotel.

At the thought, her body throbbed, not only for that taste of him she had been craving but…

For what?

Her sex responded with a long, painful twist, and she absently slid a hand over her belly.

Lust, she decided. A hunger for a joining through blood.

But she suspected it was more—a chemical reaction she had never before experienced. An addiction that could only be assuaged through Edward.

"This is ridiculous." Sam got out of his chair, rising to the full height of his rangy form—which she could see in the dark because of her heightened vision—and wandering away from the table. "Back at the hotel, you were afraid he was going to do you in, Gisele. I heard your mind reaching for me after I realized your feeding was taking way too long and started toward your room. If I hadn't gotten within mind-distance of you, as weak as you were, what would've happened?"

"He would have slain me."

Sam shook his head at her nonchalance. "So your solution is to truss Edward up and pretend that's going to cool his temper? He's ticked, and he's only going to get worse."

She picked up the pencil she had intended to use to jot down future places to visit after their business here was done. So far, the list was blank, and she jabbed the lead at the emptiness of the paper.

"I will not kill my created, Sam." The notion pierced her, and she rubbed a hand over her arm. "That would be an abomination."

During the ensuing pause, a wind moaned through

the cracks in the old planked walls, but it sounded like a cry to Gisele's sharp hearing. Ragged curtains flapped in that breeze, rustling motes of dust that eventually settled to the wooden floors.

Her companion planted his hands on his hips, leaning back against the rusted kitchen sink. "Why you didn't just kill Edward after he murdered Fegan, I'll never understand. Instead, you had to go and exchange with the bastard."

The reminder of how his blood had filled her to ecstasy made her pulsate all over. It had been the only time she had felt as if she would never be alone again.

"From what the gang had said about Edward," she murmured, "I knew that taking away his humanity would hurt him more than putting an end to his life. At the time, such a punishment for killing our creator seemed just."

"And that reckoning worked out really well, didn't it?"

Gisele drew a box on the paper, then embellished until it became a theater screen that would show any movie she wished to see. It almost made her want to go back to those days as a young woman who would stare at the screen and ponder the existential imagery and lessons about life she would never experience herself.

As a human, she had analyzed; it was only as a vampire that she had learned to participate.

And it was the theater that had brought both worlds together.

She scribbled her picture into oblivion, but it did not obscure a niggle that had come to settle in the back of her mind.

"What do they say about us becoming our own parents in the end?" she asked. "Sam, have I followed in the footsteps of the vampire who turned *me?*"

Her partner watched her carefully, his blue eyes piercing. "What do you mean?"

She pressed the pencil to paper until the lead broke. Flashes of the night she'd been turned took her over: the dark man sitting next to her as *Orphée* by Jean Cocteau played on the screen. The other film lover sliding his hand onto her chair's cushion, whispering to her in broken sentences she did not quite understand, although she had still listened raptly, not realizing back then that he had been using his voice to sway and soothe her.

But she had been willing, all the same, transfixed by the images on the screen and his words.

When he had eased his fingers under her dress, she had not even protested. And when he had bitten her, then persuaded her to exchange blood, he had put her into a weakened stupor that led her eventually to stumble out of the theater and into the night….

"As you recall, Sam," she said, "after I bit Edward, I left him, just as my own creator left me. The parallel is…unsettling…to say the least."

"It's not the same."

"Yes, it is." She flicked the pencil away. "My creator was laughing as he left me there in my seat with the film playing on and with the taste of his blood in my mouth and the sting of his bite on my neck. Laughing, as if he had perpetuated a joke. Was he getting back at someone by initiating me? I used *my* bite on Edward for a more direct revenge, but still…"

Her partner narrowed his eyes. "Good gravy, you're as philosophical as Edward was when he ran with the gang."

His name shivered over her skin like goose bumps.

"Surely you have become the same, Sam," she said. "It happened to all the older vampires: the second-guessing, the longing for more than what we gained with the exchange."

He did not say anything.

Gisele stood, running her hands down her red dress to smooth it out. "We have so much time on our hands that I suspect there is nothing else to do *but* think."

"And enjoy," Sam added too quickly.

"And…enjoy." Gisele sampled the word, but it did not hold the same strength of flavor as it had before Edward. Why? Blood had been everything—her opiate, her balm, her elixir.

"At any rate," Sam said, "unlike your own creator, you *had* to leave Edward—especially before the rest of the gang recovered from Fegan's death. Even as new humans, they could have used weapons against you if they'd decided to take Edward's side instead of yours. You had no idea where their allegiances were."

True. Most of the gang had missed Edward after he had first left them and Fegan had banned him from ever returning. Certainly, the rogue vampire had committed atrocious crimes that had put them all on alert, but Gisele suspected that the boys generally sympathized with Edward's dislike of Fegan. She had seen how their attitudes had altered toward their leader decade by decade.

But Sam definitely had not felt the same. He had immediately caught her before she left the scene that night, begging her to give him "his vampire" back. So she had taken him with her, an ally and a comfort as she had mourned her surrogate father and cursed his murderer.

Sam continued. "So bottom line? This is a good time to kill Edward—not to keep him chained up and seething."

She walked over to Sam so she could tweak him under the chin. "It is not so black and white, my friend."

"Yeah, I think it is."

"There are choices." Gisele glanced toward the ceiling, toward the attic where Edward was chained up.

At the thought, her fangs prodded her gums, extending in arousal…and perhaps in a plea for connection?

"Choices?" Sam sounded dubious.

"A taming." Gisele held a hand to her belly, where excitement stirred, flowing downward in a slow melt. "As I said, I have a few years on Edward. More power. I am certain I can show him that this back-and-forth revenge needs to end—for both of us. If I can persuade him to accept what he is, to take joy in what we can do as vampires, perhaps he will eventually come around."

"Good luck with that."

Gisele smiled. How hard could it be to sell the glory of their kind? Of experiencing each other to the fullest, without holding back? Of living in heightened bliss beyond what any human could ever know?

She found that she was even holding her breath, hoping he would accept what she had to offer.

But then she exhaled, reminding herself that this taming was borne of survival and nothing more.

"Somehow," Sam said, "I'm thinking you don't understand how many things could go wrong." He thrust a thumb in his own direction. "As another recycled vampire, I know what Edward's going through, how he's adjusting to his regained powers. It's like he's read the instruction manual, but he can't get all the parts working yet. He's not confounded and at a loss as to what to do as a preternatural; he's going to know how to use the limited powers he's got so far."

"Then I suppose I will not know his limitations unless I test them."

Sam rolled his eyes, exasperated.

Gisele laid a hand on his shoulder. "If it should come to it, there is always your way. But I must try, even if it is just for tonight."

"I still think—"

"He is my responsibility," she said.

With that, Gisele walked out of the kitchen. After a moment, her partner muttered a foul word and darted ahead of her toward the rickety, folding staircase that led to the attic.

While Sam started climbing toward the door in the ceiling, she tried to think of why else she was keeping her captive around. But she had no idea how to explain it any further.

Not when it came to Edward.

EDWARD sat on the floor of the attic, his head lolling to one side, his longish hair partially obscuring his eyesight, as the silver chains weighed down his neck and wrists.

Earlier, Sam had donned the very gloves Edward had used to handle the silver, then bolted the chains to the wall to prevent an escape.

As if that would happen, with him so drained and list-less, on the edge of an exhausted sleep he was deter-mined to avoid.

He struggled to keep his eyes open, even though the temptation to remove himself from reality was strong. Instead, he kept his mind busy by concentrating on the army of objects in this attic—remnants from someone's anonymous, abandoned life.

Through his hair, he could barely see a dust-caked organ in one corner, and it made Edward think of Sun-day mornings when he would escort his sickly mother to their country church. It was true that the congregation would whisper around them—the whore chambermaid who had fallen into bed with the duke sitting alongside her bastard son, both of whom had been turned out and denied. Yet those Sundays had been peaceful for his mother all the same because he had always defended her from the gossip with practiced, lethal glares that dared the populace to say a word in front of him.

Numerous scraps later, they had all learned to leave her be.

His gaze traveled to another object—a dressmaker's dummy clothed in a shawl that had slipped off one shoulder—and he was reminded of how he'd once tugged the dresses off women when he'd been a human. He'd had so many, but loved none.

And, as a vampire, he had refrained from taking any more. Biting kept him satiated, and to couple the act with sex would have been…

He quickly passed by the dummy, not wishing to dwell on how sex plus a bite made him feel too much like the monster he despised.

His eyes landed upon a crystal chandelier splayed on the floor and seemingly held together by spiderwebs. It spoke of grace and elegance—a higher class Edward had tried so hard to claim as his own by training himself to act like a gentleman….

The chandelier blurred as he recalled human days spent dreaming of the moment he would confront his noble-born father, showing him how polished he had become through self-education, even though he was merely a bastard banished to the country where he and his mother lived with her scowling brother.

But Edward's dreams had never materialized. He had never deemed himself good enough to present himself and, before he ever could, he had been swept into Fegan's gang. There, he'd attempted to lose himself in a new, supposedly superior existence.

Attempted and failed.

And after enduring centuries of growing to hate himself and his existence more and more, he had finally decided to seek redemption through becoming human again....

His lazy musing was interrupted by the faint sound of stairs creaking, then the click of the trapdoor in the floor opening.

Sam appeared, gifting Edward with a glare as he swung the door to the ground. He was wearing the gloves again, and they seemed right at home with his long-sleeved Henley shirt and khaki pants.

The ruffian—because that was how Edward would always see the former New York street thug—stepped into the attic, then held out his hand toward the opening.

A long, slim arm appeared out of the hole, red-lacquer-tipped fingers entwining with Sam's.

Edward's gut clenched with pure lust. The carnal response enflamed his temper—and his entire body.

In the next instant, Gisele emerged, looking every bit as desirable as all the fantasies he'd wrestled, her red dress clinging, leech-like to every streamlined curve...

Proving to her that she would never affect him, Edward tilted a careless grin at her, and her eyes widened ever so slightly.

So the captor was susceptible to a mere grin, eh?

His blood hammered through him, nailing every cell.

Hatred, he thought. *That is the reason for your passion. Remember that.*

Fortified by the reminder, he forced himself to brush a gaze over her.

She smiled now, giving him as good as she was getting.

"Hello, Edward," she said, French-pussycat lethal. "Are you well settled?"

"For a prisoner," he said, "I suppose I am rather comfortable."

Sam stepped closer to Edward. "If it was up to me, I'd drill you right now. You tried to destroy our family with those rogue attacks, and you robbed me of the existence I loved before Gisele gave it back. So don't tempt me."

"Somehow," Edward said, sinking even lower against the wall, "I suspect I lack the energy to do even that. Do you know what it's like to wear silver, Sam? If not, we can remedy the situation."

When Sam tensed up, Gisele strove to calm him with a touch to his arm. A look passed between them, and Sam hefted out a sigh, then turned around and walked toward the circular window across the room. Night shrouded the panes, and a tree branch waved in the strangled wind.

Unruffled, Gisele addressed Edward. "Just to make it clear—I am not here to kill you."

"Naturally. Why kill when torture is so much more amusing?"

Sam started to mutter, but Gisele held up a hand and, without the other vampire even seeing the gesture, he grew silent.

"These chains are not torture," she said. "They are a precaution."

Sam spoke up. "Since you can't control yourself, we're doing it for you."

"Cheers then," Edward said.

That clearly brought Sam to his limits. He faced Gisele. "You're going to tolerate him?"

She sent him another look indicating that they had talked about this before. At the same time, Edward knew that they were communicating mentally using their creator-to-created link.

Sam must not have liked what she was telling him because he yanked off his gloves and handed them to her.

"I can't stay around," he said, heading toward the attic door.

The fact that he was leaving her alone with Edward revealed just how confident they were in Gisele's abilities to handle matters. Yet that would not stop Edward if he saw an opportunity to destroy her.

He would *not* hesitate next time.

As Sam disappeared from the room, Gisele donned the gloves as if they were high-fashion accessories.

"Edward, Edward," she said.

Each time she purred his name, he grew hard.

Harder.

He stirred, his mind warring with his body. But she seemed to recognize his stimulation, her gaze lighting on his groin.

She sighed, coming closer, her high, saucy heels tapping on the floor. "Why do you wish to kill me when you want me so badly?"

"I—"

"No denials. I can hear the blood racing through you. Vampire to vampire, I can sense the change in your body, how it is readying itself for me. I greatly interest you in a way that has nothing to do with slaying, and you cannot tell me any differently."

He knew this was a losing battle, so he laconically shrugged.

She cocked her head, reading him—a powerful surge against his skull told him that much. But even with the silver, he was still able to block her from entering.

Yet he didn't know how long that would last as the energy ebbed out of him with every building pulse.

When she stopped, he breathed easier. But then she crossed her arms over her chest, the gesture pushing her small, firm breasts into succulent globes, and once again, it was hard to get air into his lungs.

"What shall I do with you?" she asked more to herself than him.

"We both know the answer to that."

"Edward." She came closer, bringing with her the scent of blood under skin—a heady fragrance that tempted his fangs to push against his gums. "I thought to persuade you of my good intentions. That is the reason I brought you here to our hideout. And, frankly," she added, glancing around the attic, "this is a very comfortable place. Fairly clean—because Sam and I dusted it off a bit the first night—and also off the beaten track out here in the country. We have done our best to preserve its abandoned appearance so as not to attract attention. Our close neighbor—a bachelor who lives a field away over the hill and is wonderfully susceptible to us—told us that no one has lived here for years. The occupants kept to themselves and simply left without a word to anyone."

As she neared, his fangs finally popped. He could not stop them in his weakened state.

She continued. "I would like to make things right between us. Wouldn't it be far more agreeable to come to an understanding?"

He barked out a soft laugh. That was rich.

Resting his cheek against the wall, he concentrated on shutting her out: her scent, her proximity. All of it was chiseling into him and wearing him down.

But when she came to hover only inches away, she invaded his every sense, every weakness.

"My goal," she said softly, almost tenderly, "is to tame you."

If he had possessed the energy, he would have physically struck out at her instead of only using words. "Tame? As a master would tame a wild thing?"

"You are not wild, merely…misunderstood."

"You should listen to Sam," he said, hating that he could not fight back or even fight at all. "He has sense enough to know that I will not take to any taming."

She paused, got a speculative twinkle in her gaze, then slowly lowered herself to all fours, crawling toward him until she was in his line of sight. Her erotic pose caused frenzied need to surge through him until his gaze took on a brutal red tinge that colored her every move.

Turned on…almost out of control….

"You know," she said, "the more you resist, the more you challenge me. And I do adore a challenge, Edward. Perhaps if you had stayed with the gang, you would have known that."

"I was not about to be Fegan's puppet even one more night. Pity that you cared so little for yourself or for the world that you never left him."

She tilted her head. "Stephen, Roger…all of the boys came to despise Fegan, but he was a creature of his age and appetites. In his later years, he did mellow."

Edward thought of the greedy, slothful vampire whose gaudy rings had cut into his fingers. Fegan's appetites had been so disgusting that the gang had slowly distanced themselves from his blood orgies; slowly because it would not do to offend Fegan outright, lest they pay a heavy price. But Edward had chanced it, leaving the group during the Second World War, in spite of the threat of extermination from the powerful master should he ever cross paths with Edward again.

Since Edward had not yet learned that killing his creator would free him, he'd never intended to return, anyway. The threat of extermination was a pittance compared to all the education he had absorbed, all the sights he had seen around the world as he had explored possible ways to retrieve his soul and flush away all his vampiric sins by starting over again.

Recently, during one of Edward's visits to the now-human Stephen and his family, Stephen *had* said that the only tempering influence on Fegan in his later years had been Gisele. It was true that she had accompanied the rapacious vampire on most of his blood-soaked rampages, but Stephen doubted there had been as much senseless carnage with her there to pull him back.

However, Edward had seen no proof of decency in her. Even now, he sensed that she was more animal than anything, with her feral gaze and sinuous body.

The corners of her mouth had lifted in an alluring smile, and he knew that she was dead set on this taming idea of hers.

Slowly, she reached out with a gloved hand, tugging on Edward's coat. When he didn't resist, she began to work it from his shoulders.

Anger welled in him, but he didn't move. First, she wouldn't dare bite him with the silver on him since it had poisoned his system, so that gave him some measure of defense. Also, the silver was still binding *him,* so he couldn't do much anyway.

In his present state, Gisele really did have the power to overcome him, and it seemed that his wisest option would be to bide his time until he could somehow slip out of the chains after she had gone, regain his strength, then launch a surprise attack when she returned.

Yes, he would withstand her taming for now, he thought as she unwrapped the chains from around one of his wrists. Then she guided his coat off that side, replacing the chains and repeating the process with his other arm.

Problem was, this strip-off reminded him a little too vividly of those revenge-turned-sexual fantasies he'd battled: her tearing off his shirt, his pants, then him turning the tables and dominating her, ripping her clothing off in kind….

His cock throbbed along with his fang-pierced gums.

Hate, he reminded himself. *Focus.*

"This is part of the taming, I presume," he said dryly.

His jacket was on the floor by now, as she assessed his T-shirt. With a pleased sound, she ripped the cotton down the center, then ran her gloved fingers down his chest, her eyes glowing.

A quiver contracted Edward's belly, his cock straining against his pants. But the lust was for her blood, he knew, not *her.*

It couldn't be for her.

She jerked the shirt the rest of the way off his body, taking care to keep his chains in place. Meanwhile, he inhaled her as if she were smooth, blood-laced smoke.

"You are built, for an Englishman," she said. "But as the boys used to tell it, you were working in the stables around the time Fegan discovered you. That would have given you these muscles."

He shielded himself from her lulling voice. "Does this taming involve much else but tedium?"

"Mmm," she said, circling a finger around one of his nipples and bringing it to a peak.

He fought to contain a moan because he wanted her to keep going even more than he wanted her to stop.

"So responsive," she whispered. "I anticipate a lovely experience with you after we come to terms."

Obviously mindful of the silver, Gisele leaned toward him, sniffing his skin at his temple, then lower, near his ear. She shivered, and when she spoke, her breath stirred his hair.

It tickled.

The sensation drove his anger to even greater heights.

"Everyone," she whispered, "smells so differently, do they not? And the taste of blood…different for each feeding, as well. *Your* taste, Edward, to me was like…"

She inhaled along the line of his jaw, and he shuddered, telling himself that it was out of repulsion.

His fangs—arousal at its most primitive—scratched his lips as he retorted, "Like what, Gisele? I do hope I reminded you of hemlock."

But she had already backed away on all fours, hiding her face while she rubbed it against her arm, her breath coming quick and harsh. She was reveling in what she had inhaled on his skin.

Or had she smelled the trace of silver poisoning him and retreated?

His flesh burned where she had sniffed him, and the heat spread under his skin, matching the crimson haze of his excited vision.

When she raised her head, her glowing eyes were like twin suns, her fangs poised and gleaming.

It was as if he had been stabbed in the gut—her excitement was that stimulating.

"Even a dabble brings it all back," she said, panting. "I remember our exchange, how much I wanted more."

She moved toward him, and he called on every last ounce of strength to show his true vampire face to her, hissing, hideous, a dire warning to stay away.

A desperate last move to keep himself under control because all he really wanted was to taste her again, to drink in what he'd been yearning for since that night.

But he couldn't allow her another bite—a repeat of the moment his soul had been stolen by this female vampire who had taken Fegan's place as Edward's worst enemy.

At his show of defiance, she backed away, her eyes cooling to a milder light brown, her fangs receding.

Moments passed, heartbeats marking each second.

"I…" she began, and for a strange instant, he thought she might apologize.

As his vision settled back to its normal hue, she bowed her head, sitting on her knees as she modulated her breathing. Her short, sharp hair whisked forward, moving with each exhalation.

She stayed that way for so long his body lost its will, mellowing to his non-attack form, the silver draining him in earnest once again.

Still, as long as she was close, he couldn't help scenting her, imagining her under *him* as he tasted her skin, bit into it, sucked….

When she finally looked up, she did seem regretful. But perhaps Edward was only misinterpreting that. He had spent so much time wandering, studying the nature of the world and what might lie beyond it, that he often bequeathed emotions to things that couldn't possibly feel them. Trees sang in the wind for him, although the tunes were often sad. The moon seemed lonely in its isolated perch in the sky.

And he was no doubt doing the same here, with Gisele.

She tilted her head at him again, and something in his stomach flipped.

"By the end of this," she said softly, "you will understand me, Edward. You will know that I only wished to set the world to rights—and that is what I want now, more than anything. I want us to take happiness from each other instead of pain."

"You want to be my master," he said.

She didn't respond, only stood and went over to the trunk by the far wall. As she opened it, there was a groan from the hinges, then a wail when she closed it.

Much to his surprise, she took out a patchwork comforter and came to spread it over him; it smelled of gingerbread and some human's idea of what home was.

Maybe after he killed her, he would find such a home.

"You will come to see my side of this," Gisele said as she retreated to the door in the floor. "And I will see yours when you accept who you are. Who *we* are to each other."

As she disappeared and closed the door after her, Edward sank into the comforter, closing his eyes and holding on to the gingerbread smell of humanity.

A scent that masked Gisele's blood perfume and refilled him with the hatred he would need to triumph over what she did to him every time she came near.

3

SAM WANDERED under the June moonlight, his iPod turned up high as he listened to the Sex Pistols, who provided aggressive songs to fit his mood.

Even though the music blasted in his ears, he couldn't really say he heard much of it; he was still mentally tuned in to this harebrained plan of Gisele's to "tame" Edward.

Sam bent to pick up a rock from the dirt road and heave it into the surrounding oaks. He should be used to taking all kinds of orders—not only from his first gang back in what was now Lower Manhattan, where Sam had learned to con right around the time he had learned to walk, but also from Fegan and his schemes to fleece the toughest marks imaginable, whether they be in heavily guarded mansions or pious victims who didn't seem as though they'd be interested in the debauchery a vampire might offer.

But Fegan had loved to break and bloody them all, and now Gisele was being just as determined and difficult.

Taming. Why even try when Edward clearly intended to kill anyone in his path, especially Sam and Gisele, if it meant getting back his soul? He'd already proven that he was willing to do anything back in Las Vegas—the rogue vampire had taunted Fegan by draining human women to the brink of death in the hopes that the threat of vampire exposure would draw their creator out of hiding to stop it.

Sam's footsteps paced the speed of his frustration. Curse Edward anyway. Sam had never liked him, even when the other vampire had been in their gang. The brooding Brit had always been too thoughtful, too much of a burden around their ankles, weighing them down with all his book-learning about ethics and morality—concepts they didn't need as vampires, really. Edward had even influenced the other gang members—Stephen and Roger in particular—to gradually become disenchanted with Fegan and their lifestyle, and they'd all told Sam he would feel the same way some day, too.

They'd been wrong about that. If anything, Sam loved what he was more with each passing decade. The only thing he'd agreed with Stephen about was the necessity of remaining unattached to the humans. But then Stephen had gone and fallen for one of them, and after Fegan's murder, had lost everything when he'd regained a soul, as far as Sam was concerned.

He rounded a corner where the tremble of a rushing river cut the night. Humidity brushed his skin, but the insects that might've been drawn to the sweaty lure of mortal flesh kept their distance.

Even they knew that Sam wasn't human—and thank you very much for that. He'd just as soon forget those years of living as an orphan in flophouses, scratching out a living on the streets, watching his older brother and partner get knifed in a disagreement over a freakin' chunk of bread.

Who wanted to go back to *that*...?

Something stopped Sam in his tracks. A human scent carried on the foliage-laden air.

He leaned back his head, taken by the sweetness, warm and sticky as newly spun taffy. A pulse—not his own—tapped against his chest, seeking entrance.

Pausing his iPod to silence his music, Sam heard it: the alluring stomp of a heartbeat.

Human blood. Under all the sweetness, he scented it now.

He followed the vital signs along the road, hearing and smelling and feeling over the roll of the river, the freshness of the vegetation.

The aroma grew stronger just as he came to the blue bridge, a local landmark that spanned the water and stood, stoic under the moonlight.

But what Sam saw on that bridge made him hesitate.

A young woman balanced on a side rail, arms spread wide, face lifted to the moon as she walked to the end of the structure. In the stretch of a moment, he saw her as a sheer outline—almost as if she blended with the night and air.

Then more details: ample curves filling out a light-blue summer dress. Dark hair tightly curled to her shoulders. Cocoa skin, making him think she was what a white guy like him would've once called mulatto back in his human days when he didn't know any better.

She seemed to cant to the side, as if losing her equilibrium, threatening to fall to the rocky water below. And even though he had feasted earlier in the night, her scent still enthralled Sam enough to instinctively set him into motion.

Blood—all he could think about was saving her blood—

With the speed of a knife flying through the air, he zoomed from the trees and over the bridge, coming to her and wrapping an arm around her waist then whipping her off the rail and to the ground. As she fell toward the steel, he slowed their momentum, cushioning her with his arms, a strange cradle that kept her unhurt.

In the breath-choked aftermath, their gazes met, and he saw the bottomless pools of darkness that were her eyes.

Time seemed to suspend as they stared at each other, her gasping, him recovering.

Recovering from what, he didn't know.

Before he could stop himself, he'd glanced into her with a superficial reading; he'd need to touch her temple if he wanted to go deeper, but all he wanted to know was why she was alone at this time of night, here, on a bridge.

In a flash, he saw her waiting for a man who would come to pick her up in a car, just as he had on other nights, when she'd snuck away from her roommates, who disapproved of the guy. It was their secret meeting place close to her home, but the man hadn't shown up tonight and she was still waiting, telling herself he would come, getting bored while doing so.

She'd walked bridge rails since she was young, so she'd hopped on up, killing time....

Stephen's old philosophy—before he'd gone human again—slapped at Sam and he stopped reading her.

Never get involved.

Yeah, that's what Stephen had preached, and he'd been older than Sam by over a hundred years, and he was that much wiser, too. There'd been a time when the elder vampire had known the agony of loving one of them—Cassandra, a belle from Savannah—and it had left him bereft. Sam had seen how the pain had hounded Stephen long after the doomed romance had ended, and he had taken the lesson seriously, even after Stephen had broken his own promises and loved a second mortal woman, Kimberly.

They will destroy you, was what Stephen used to tell Sam back when he'd been in full possession of his logic. *Drink from them and then forget. It is as easy as that.*

Disconnecting had never been hard for Sam. After all, it'd been that way for him as a human.

He let go of the young woman, easing her the rest of the way to the ground and backing away. He should get out of here before she asked where he'd come from or how he'd been so quick in saving her or why it'd felt so weird when he'd looked into her eyes.

"Oh, your hands are cold," she said.

Yeah—out of here *now.* Before she realized that his skin covered a physical hardness that wasn't quite human.

But, as he pulled back, she gripped his arm. "Wait."

Her strength surprised him, gave him pause. Little by little, the moonlight revealed more nuances: the creamy dark shade of her skin, the slight freckles dusting her nose, the long lashes framing her brown eyes.

But there was something about her…. A fey quality that he couldn't fathom.

She looked at her hand banding his arm, then laughed—a quavering sound. She'd started to shake, and Sam could sense the adrenaline flooding her now.

"Whoa." She exhaled and slumped to the ground, staring at the sky, laughing again.

The vibrations traveled through him, a buzz that made him half drunk.

He cleared his throat. "I…didn't want you to fall."

She pushed herself to a sitting position and sent him a shocked glance. "Fall?"

Sam furrowed his brow, not knowing what to make of her.

"I've been balancing on bridge rails like that since I was…I guess about rail-high," she said. "And I've never fallen before."

She almost sounded offended in that Kentucky accent that he liked to listen to just about as much as the other music that entertained him nowadays. He guessed it even calmed him more than hearing the Sex Pistols' rage.

"Oh," was all he said, suddenly feeling like a jackass.

"Hate to erase your chivalrous moment."

"You didn't."

"Good. Because it's just a thing I do, walking, balancing, thinking things over."

Sam wondered if she was regretting meeting that man here before. Sounded like it.

He'd sensed that she was a happy person save for the basic human neuroses. But there'd been a well-hidden dark streak in her, too; she was a human who enjoyed looking into shady places—like the dangerous currents of a river—and wondering what was beneath the surface.

Sam distanced himself. She was only one of *them*— a possible blood source.

The young woman had narrowed her eyes while watching him. "You're pretty fast. I didn't even see or hear you coming."

Leave now, he told himself, just as quickly as he'd come. Now.

Now.

But he didn't move a muscle. Nope, instead he found himself blocking off his senses so her blood wouldn't stir his hunger. He didn't need the sustenance tonight, anyway, seeing as he was full from his earlier meal.

"You were kind of in your own little world," he said. "I made plenty of noise."

"You did?"

He noted how, as she stared at him, her shock seemed to be wearing off. She was just realizing that she was in the middle of nowhere with a male stranger who might not turn out to be a hero after all.

"Just be more careful," he said, standing.

He wasn't hungry, he kept telling himself. That's why he was leaving without getting a taste of her. When it was time to eat tomorrow, maybe he would come back and see if she was here again. It'd be an easy meal, and it beat hunting at the bars and dance clubs. Besides, tonight's take from the wallet he'd filched would last him and Gisele the rest of the week, so there was no need for another run to the city if he could eat here in the country.

The idea of reserving her for the next meal really did appeal, so he nudged the young woman with his sway. Using his mind, he let her know that she had no reason to be afraid of him while tacitly insinuating that she should be here tomorrow night—when he *would* be hungry.

He soothed her with his voice, too. "So, you're okay? Or should I walk you home, or…?"

Wow, he sounded like some kind of gentleman. That was a hoot.

"I can manage." She was giving him a level look now, and he knew the only reason she wasn't more afraid was because he was mentally manipulating her. "Who are you, anyway, walking around here this late?"

"I'm…"

Who? What? If he wanted her back here tomorrow, he'd have to play it safe.

"I'm kind of an insomniac," he said, the lie all too easy. "I'm staying with a cousin, and I couldn't get to sleep, so I thought a walk—"

"Where are you from?"

Even with the aid of his sway, she was so friendly it astounded Sam. Her openness actually reminded him of the one real girlfriend he'd had as a mortal—a fellow street rat named Molly. They'd popped each other's cherries when they were in their early teens—yeah, very romantic—then drifted apart. But that wasn't surprising, seeing as his existence had been one continual drift.

To answer this female's question, he pulled a story out of his mental hat, keeping his tale simple. That was always important in a con. "I come from Lexington. Not too far away, but I'm a city boy and I'm still getting used to the backwoods out here."

"Backwoods." She stood, brushing off her skirt. "Don't tell me you're one of those condescending city snobs. We have neighbors out here who actually went to college and all that fancy stuff, you know."

Her tone was gently chiding; there was a degree of pride beneath it.

Now that she was standing, he looked her over again, noticing that she only came up to his shoulder. Everything about her was lush, from her figure to her wild hair to the darkish-creamy skin that he was trying so hard to shut out.

"I didn't mean to insult you," he said.

"All right, then."

She checked him out thoroughly, too, clearly not ashamed to be so interested. He did his best to hide anything and everything that tagged him as…unusual.

"You off from college for the summer or something?" she asked.

"College isn't for me." Another rule of the con—try not to give a mark a story that could be paper-trailed. All he needed was for her to have a relative who worked at a local school, then he'd be in a tight spot trying to explain his way out of the lie.

"I'm not in college, either," she said, as if relieved at his confession. "After high school, I thought I might get a job in my aunt's office. She hunts down vintage cars for well-to-do customers, so I put off higher education for that. Then, before I knew it, seven years had passed and I'd never done more than take a few scattered classes at the community college." She sighed. "Time does fly, doesn't it?"

He did the arithmetic. She was probably around twenty-five, which made her five years older than he'd been when he'd gotten turned.

But other than looking young for their ages, they didn't have anything else in common. Just the blood that kept thrusting through her veins and tempting him to get close enough to smell her more thoroughly, to allow his fangs to emerge, to…

Sam swallowed, telling himself he *didn't* want to bite her. Not now—it would be wasteful and he'd spent too much time rationing food as a human ever to lose the instinct.

It occurred to him that, as a vampire, he should be looking forward to hunting. Fegan had encouraged him to enjoy the effects a bite could have on a human—making them worshipful slaves to their whims, if a vampire wished. But Sam pushed all that aside, wandering away from her instead.

Really. It was time for him to leave. But it wouldn't be amiss for him to prime her a little more for meeting him tomorrow.

"So," he said, "you hang around here often, doing your bridge thing?"

As she watched him put distance between them, her posture lost a little of its bearing. "Some nights."

"Tomorrow night?"

She perked up again, her eyes going bright. Was she that needful of company? Sam was speared with something he couldn't even start to explain—something he completely shut out.

But he thought it might be something like sympathy, which didn't do him any good at all.

"I can probably be here tomorrow night," she said, smiling.

But he knew that was because she was still under his sway. She might go home tonight and become as afraid as she should've been, then never show up at the bridge again.

At any rate, he held up his hand in an affable farewell, turning around and finally leaving her.

Hoping that she would indeed be there so he wouldn't have to hunt by himself while Gisele tamed Edward.

Gisele had been busy while Edward slept; she had used her preternatural grace and speed to haul bucketful after bucketful of water from an on-property creek to the attic so she could fill the antique clawfoot tub she had found a few nights ago.

A sensuous bath was the next step in her plan to persuade Edward to accept their natural bond—the primal link between creator and created.

But Gisele also wondered if it went even beyond

that. If she was making the attempt to keep him from rejecting her as she had been rejected: by her own creator, even by her human parents.

As she was pouring the final bucket of liquid into the tub, he awakened, setting their bond to sizzling.

The aroma of his blood snared her once more, like a scent that had been composed only for her. She should not be so hungry though, because during Edward's slumber, she had taken care to summon and feed from the friendly neighbor just over the hill—a strapping young fellow who kept harness-racing horses on the property adjacent to this one.

Terrence Gorley was a simple man, highly open to her mind tricks and perfectly willing to accommodate her appetite. The only reason she had not entertained the notion of staying here in this old house and feeding off the bachelor for an extended period of time was that she did not allow attachments to humans; Sam operated under the same rules, so it had made their companionship all the easier.

Gisele wished she had fed from Terrence earlier, as the longing for blood had cost her with Edward. She had wanted to drink from him—and only him—so badly that her need had muddled her logic, and she had gotten carried away during their first taming session.

But that would not happen again, now that she was properly fed. She was certain of it.

Running her hand through the mild water, she glanced at her created, finding that he was perusing the ruffled, thin, knee-length dressing gown she had donned for her bath.

A delicious quake tingled all over her. Vampire or not, Edward's combination of ruggedness and courtliness would have captured her interest even as a human. She would have wanted to skim her fingertips down his face, mapping those beautiful cheekbones. Would have loved to feel his smooth muscles under her palms and lips.

When he saw that she had caught him looking, he raised an eyebrow in a So-I'm-only-male gesture. Then he summoned enough energy to push off the floor and prop himself against the wall.

She would get him to admit that he wanted this existence.

That would be the first true step in taming him.

"Morning, my sunshine," she said.

A hank of longish hair fell over half his face, obscuring his eyes as he sat wrapped in the comforter.

"So you aren't a nightmare after all," he said lightly.

She smiled. "Do you know how many males—both human and vampire—would kill to receive my attentions?"

"Pity the poor nutters."

Having expected this feistiness, Gisele strolled to Edward, first picking up the gloves from the center of the floor and sliding them over her hands. Then, she worked the comforter off him, exposing his bare chest and pausing to run a hand over the muscles of his arm, enjoying every bulge.

She felt him quiver, but she did not mock him for that. Not when her belly was clenching in a mass of knots and tightening to the point where she had to contain a few shivers herself.

Backing away, she removed the gloves. "I do love to look at you."

"I'm afraid that taking away my shirt has nothing to do with 'looking at me' and everything to do with breaking me down. What comes next—my trousers?"

She tapped a bare finger against her mouth. "I believe I will leave that up to you. Because you *will* want them off when you are ready to accept what we can have together."

She was talking about enhancing the taste of blood with sex, a combination that brought a vampire an almost animal pleasure. A mere bite was necessary for food, for control. But coupled with sex, it was explosive.

And, oh, *how* explosive it would be with the two of them. Already, Gisele was throbbing with the new sensations only he provided.

He laughed at her suggestion, the mocking sound a wordless message that he would never be content with vampire relations when there was so much more to human sex that he could discover if he had his soul. If he was allowed another chance at all humanity had to offer.

But Gisele knew what his show of defiance hid. His pounding body, his every vital sign, told her that he was wrestling with himself. She *had* to persuade him that she could give him so much more than a return to mortality ever could.

She resolutely continued her plan, delicately stepping into the tub one foot after the other and lowering herself into the water.

Her gown floated on the surface as she sat against the high back, her hands resting on the rim. The water had already soaked through the material, sticking to her breasts.

And Edward could not keep his eyes off them.

Her nipples hardened under his attention and she allowed her knees to part, furthering the tease. The water smacked against the tub, lapping, playing.

"You're certainly pulling out all the stops," Edward finally said.

"I like baths." She dipped her fingers in the water, waving them around. "Don't you have an indulgence or two? Or are you so wound up all the time that you never relax?"

"You'd be wound up, as well, if you had a purpose like mine."

The statement struck her as interesting. "But I do have a purpose. I intend to win you over. Is that not a mission you can respect?"

"I'm afraid it's a useless one, dear."

"And why is that?"

She coasted one hand over a knee, then down her thigh. The only sounds in the attic were the lyrical rush of the wind through the old walls, the rustle of willow branches outside, the water licking at the tub, the quickened breathing of her captive.

"Edward?" she asked, cajoling.

"You don't need an explanation from me."

It seemed as if he had let down his guard slightly, and she saw this as a tiny improvement.

One step at a time.

"I cannot help thinking," she said, "that if we had met in another era, another place, we might have gotten on much better than this." She rubbed her thigh, knowing he would be able to hear the friction, even if he had forced himself to glance away.

"I doubt that. Besides all the obvious reasons for abhorring you, we have little in common."

"Do you think that a more modern girl such as I and a stuffy old man such as you could never have a meeting of the..." She slid her hand lower. "...minds?"

He gritted his teeth, but his tone was nonchalant. "Years of warring between the Brits and the French have proved that we don't mix. Then add the fact that you ruined my life and we've got ourselves a definitive answer."

She knew he would not be tamed all in one night—the challenge might even take months—but his tenacity still pinched at her. However, the frustration only encouraged her to push on.

Plus, whether he realized it or not, she had gotten him to actually converse with her.

"Perhaps," she said, lazily raising her arms over her head and resting them on the back of the tub, "a woman of my tastes might find you too crusty anyway."

His gaze went directly to her breasts again. The linen of her gown was like a second, sexy skin.

Her nipples tingled for his touch—the sensation so heightened she almost winced. But why him? What did he do to her that no other had ever managed?

"I was what one might call a 'cinema snob' in my younger years," she said. "I spent nights in the theaters watching films that my parents would hate, films that enlightened me and, truthfully, made me feel intellectually superior to others. Then a select crowd of us would go to the cafés and discuss film theory and symbolism until the sun rose. Afterward, I would go home with a fellow intellectual—a university professor or a graduate student who smoked too many cigarettes and lectured on such matters as *la Nouvelle Vague*—the French New Wave—while I hung on his every word."

"Sounds rather pretentious to me," Edward said, once again raising a casual eyebrow.

"Yes," she said, "I suppose I was a cliché. So enamored with the image I had cultivated. I was very young and silly."

Edward did not answer, and she took the moment to

consider him. Devastatingly handsome, and he still looked so young, too, even with all the folly of his mis-spent years coloring his amber eyes. How old had he been when he was turned the first time—twenty-nine? Thirty?

She allowed her hands to slide down the top of the tub and over her hair, wetting it. Then she caressed her face, her jaw…her neck.

Edward's amber gaze flared golden.

Once again, she relived his taste: addictive, like something delectably juicy.

She coaxed her hands over her breasts, her stomach, her belly. His chest heaved for breath, even as he attempted to control himself.

When she reached between her legs, she shifted, and water spilled over the side of the tub to the floor, smacking the wood, the sound reverberating through the quiet room.

"Stop it, Gisele," he growled, low and menacing.

She groaned, propping one foot on the edge while grabbing the other side with one hand. Half-closing her eyes, she sketched a finger up through the folds of her sex until she came to her clit. She pressed there, massaging and wiggling her hips.

She thought she heard him strangle a common curse, but he was not looking away this time.

"What if I got out of this tub," she whispered, "and came straight over to you, Edward? What would you do with me?"

His fevered pulse heated the very air in the room, and that was enough of an answer. However, a hint of fang also told her that he might kill her if she ever got too close.

Closing her eyes all the way now, she pictured a more

appealing scenario: climbing out of the tub, her gown spilling water to the floor as she came to him. Lifting the drenched material over her hips, offering herself, and him grabbing her, pulling her to his mouth, then sliding down her with his lips to work her with his tongue.

He would ravish her, gnaw at her, but take care not to draw blood until he had tugged her down to his lap, then pierced her neck with his fangs, accepting her.

As the fantasy played out like the most vivid of films on a screen, she slid a finger inside herself. She was swollen, wet, ready. At the same time, she circled her thumb around her clit until she was making little sighing noises.

Vaguely, she heard Edward's heartbeat matching time with hers, as if she had found a lost half of herself; his breathing even shuddered through her as surely as if it were her own.

Every thrust of his presence into her brought her to a higher level of slick ecstasy. She inserted a second finger into her passage, straining until a heavier wave slopped out of the tub.

High, so high…higher…

She heard Edward moan first and she echoed him—his moan like her own, traveling her lungs, her limbs in a shared build-up.

The moan turned to a cry, then a scream that climaxed into a thousand dots of color that composed a bigger picture.

Her fangs bit into the tender skin of her lower lip, paining her back to reality.

Slowly, she opened her eyes to find Edward in the same slouched position as she was, their bodies imitating each other in every way.

Never before, she thought. She had never come so hard, and there had not even been a bite involved.

He opened his eyes, too, embers of the shared orgasm in his gaze, chest rising up and down.

Perhaps it was the afterglow, but Gisele found herself reaching a hand out to him, as if he might accept her now that they had connected in this inexplicable way.

A way that warped her emotions in circles, making her mind still whirl.

But when Edward clenched his jaw, closed his eyes and turned his gaze away, Gisele felt as if her hand had been slapped.

Jilted, she slowly sat back up, trying to hide the surprising decimation that was taking her apart limb by limb.

And when Edward spoke, it was all she could do to stop from dying inside.

"Maybe you've weakened me," he said. "But it's only because you're just as poisonous as this silver."

He held up a hand, his chains dangling, then allowed it to drop to his side again.

Leaving Gisele weakened, too.

4

As EDWARD drank in the sight of Gisele in that bathtub, he tried to enjoy the bruised expression on her face. In the afterburn of their climax, his breath came short and shallow, his body tingling as if trying to reform.

But even in the throes of hurting his creator—a victory, for all intents and purposes—he couldn't bring himself to gloat.

Was it because her reaction had thrown him off guard? Or was it because taking a jab at her didn't hold a fraction of the contentment it should have?

Why had hurting her backfired on him instead?

He searched for an answer, coming up empty. But this was precisely why he needed his humanity back. With it, he was sure to discover all the answers that had eluded him for so long. There had to be more to "life" than he had already found, and without all the carnal distractions of vampirism, he could come down to earth again—he would see so much more clearly. Even before he had been turned, he had longed for something…anything…to complete him, and perhaps with a few more mortal years, he would've found it.

Little had he known that, centuries later, he would still be at a loss as to just what that something was.

Yet, when Gisele had invited him to enjoy her beauty,

her erotic show, he *had* been attracted to what she offered. With her—a being so much like him, a creature
trying to make up for what she'd done—he had been
able to let himself go, even if just for a body-thunder-
ing moment.

Did she, too, understand what it was like to be unde-
serving? She knew darkness but seemed to have found
a way out of it—a way he'd never considered.

He chopped off this train of thought, unwilling even
to contemplate that anything but regaining his humanity
would bring fulfillment. With his soul, he would appreciate each numbered day. He would be saved.

Drawing the blanket tighter around him, he floated
down from the last of his high, the colors of the attic going from red to regular night tones, his fangs receding.

Some stickiness on his trousers reminded him that he
had come, but he schooled himself to seem distant, un-
affected, even as he fought off lingering images of his
enemy in the bathtub, working herself—working *him*—
to a spiraling explosion.

Gisele clearly had recovered, having submerged herself all the way, then coming back up again, her hair and
skin water-steeped. Then, using the soap she had earlier
placed on a tray, she lathered herself after removing the
thin linen gown.

The aroma of wildflowers intoxicated Edward, reminding him of earthy days in the country when he had
been a boy. In the meadows, where he exercised the
horses, he had forgotten about all the ugly words his
mother and her brother would exchange at the meal table.

I'll not have that bastard in my house another day,
the man would say, continuing with his tirade even after
Edward entered the cottage after finishing his labors.

Please, George, his mum, withered before her time, would answer. *Just abide by us until we present ourselves to his father....*

A day that had never arrived.

Gisele had by now dunked herself again to wash her hair and skin clear of suds. She came up, water sluicing down her gamine face until she smoothed back her hair. Then she stood, a deluge steaming from her firm breasts tipped by those cherried nipples. Dragging his gaze farther downward, Edward took in her tiny waist, flat stomach, slim hips, then the dark thatch of hair between her legs.

Edward's loins seized, but he commanded himself to overcome her allure.

To forget that he'd felt so close to her.

However, she obviously knew better, her lips tipping up at the corners.

"Are you hungry yet, Edward?" she asked.

He had kept himself from thinking about that. "I'm fine."

"When did you last drink?"

"Earlier last night." A flash of an arched neck, a woman's gasp, came back to him.

Gisele seemed to consider this. Her experience would tell her that he would have hunger pangs by the next time dusk settled over the horizon.

How he was going to manage meals while chained to a wall, he had no idea. But Edward could withstand an amazing amount of adversity if it meant achieving success.

Negligently, his captor donned her wet gown and wrung out the bottom, allowing most of it to cling to her body.

Taunting woman. Once he got a hold of her…

What?

What exactly would he do?

She stepped out of the tub, droplets shivering to the floor. His lungs constricted as if he was being smothered by a thick pillow.

"Tell me," she said. "What was your last meal like?"

Recalling how feral Gisele herself had been earlier, just after she had chained him, Edward wondered when *she* had last eaten, whether she was asking him this because she wanted some vicarious satisfaction from the image of him feeding. Then again, a seasoned vampire such as she had probably found some blood before her bath, because she didn't have that air of wild appetite about her anymore.

Still, he couldn't deny himself the opportunity to taunt her just as she had done to him.

"I found my last prey just after dusk," he said, locking gazes with her, mainly in an effort to ignore her body. "A hitchhiker who will never recall meeting me in a coffee shop's parking lot."

"A woman?" Gisele whispered, her eyes burning voraciously. He was right—she was getting off on this.

"Females who take well to being soothed are my preference."

"Even when you went rogue, they were willing?"

Trying to fire him up, was she? "After being swayed in a proper manner, most humans always are willing. You would know this. But I assume you like more of a challenge than that presents."

"You assume wrong."

She turned her back on him, wandering away from the tub while tracing her long, graceful fingers along its edges. The damp gown molded to her ass, making it seem as round and smooth as summer fruit.

Juices stung Edward's mouth. He swallowed.

"So tell me," Gisele continued, taking up where he had left off. "Did you whisper to this little hitchhiker that you saw her across the parking lot and wanted to kiss her more than anything? Did you maneuver her into a dark, quiet place and moan sweet nothings into her ear as you worshipped her body with your mouth until it came time for the bite?"

At the muted escalation of her heartbeat, Edward sensed that it was a proper time to take her lascivious enjoyment away, like a treat rescinded from a naughty girl.

He got technical, draining any color from his description. "Soothing masks their memories and allows us to survive in secrecy. What other way would you have me treat prey?"

Gisele came to the big window on the opposite wall, pressing her hands against a pane as she stared at the branch-gnarled darkness. She cast no reflection.

"You hardly sound as cruel as the reputation you cultivated as the rogue," she said.

"Cruel?" he asked, his ire rising once again. He used it to chase away the sight of her skin through that gown, used it to erase the recollection of all the very necessary sins he had committed in his quest to kill Fegan. "I didn't delight in biting those women. I did what I had to in order to rid the world and myself of Fegan. But I'm curious, Gisele. What is *your* definition of the word *cruel?*"

"The same as yours. The same as any one of the vampires in our old gang."

"Doubtful." He leaned forward, his chains stirring. "Fegan had an entirely different concept of cruelty. After I left him, I met others like me. There are a number of particularly *civil* masters out there."

"Fegan did relish his blood sport." She leaned her entire body against the window, pressing a cheek to the glass while glancing back at him. "But he did enjoy his reputation even more—it caused other master vampires to respect him."

"What are you saying?"

Gisele's forehead creased in thought. "He would know when he was going too far. At least when I was with him."

"All the others did say you were able to keep the glutton in check."

Gisele turned all the way back around. "Pardon me, but did you just offer a semi-positive comment about me?"

Edward inclined his head in acknowledgment. Yes, it seemed that he had.

"I wasn't insinuating that you were any kind of guardian angel," he added. "Merely that you seemed to have some effect on a creature that couldn't possibly get any worse."

"Of course. I understand that you will never, under any circumstances, compliment me."

But she smiled to herself, then bent her head as she wrung more water out of her gown. The liquid tap, tap, tap on the wood planks was a welcome relief for his senses, especially since her smile had plunged a bolt of brightness through him.

She leaned back against the window.

Breasts, so firm and rounded, the material sheer over them…

Focus, man, focus.

Edward summoned back the hatred, plus a fair amount of ye olde self-disgust, and that did the trick.

Her good nature dissipated, a wistful sort of expression taking its place. He had no idea why she would try with such tenacity to tame him. Wouldn't it benefit her to do away with the threat he presented?

She meandered to a nearby trunk, flipping it open and setting a cloud of dust to the air. Waving a hand in front of her face, she coughed and said, "Understand—I am not defending Fegan's appetites. I accepted long ago that they were overkill. He did not have self-control, but he was at his best when someone was around to give it to him— someone who appreciated what he had done for them."

Like *her?*

"In fact," she added, "he reminded me of a young boy who goes away to university and explores his new freedoms a touch too intensely."

"Boys normally grow up. Most of them even develop a conscience."

Gisele cocked her head. "A vampire with a conscience. Most say that is the stuff of fiction."

"You knew creatures like Stephen and Roger well enough," he said, referring to his brethren. "They knew which lines not to cross. Why didn't you?"

"I…" She shook her head. "I have learned."

As if not knowing what else to do, she began rifling through the trunk.

She was fooling herself, he thought. Gisele was no more than a mindless creature, a slave to her vampire.

After searching—gathering her composure, he would wager—she pulled out a length of red-and-orange silk that she rubbed against her cheek in sensuous appreciation.

For a taboo moment, he became the silk against her skin, skimming it and causing wonderful friction.

She's your enemy, he repeated again and again.

Gisele hugged the material to her chest. "You are never going to believe anything but the worst about

Fegan, and from what you saw of him in the old days with his blood orgies, I cannot blame you. But you, yourself, have maintained that vampires do learn and adapt throughout the years. They can change their states of mind, their attitudes. Why would this not be true of Fegan, even though he might have considered this a weakness and downplayed it in front of the gang?"

"You would know since you seem to have been his only confidante."

"I suppose I was. He never needed to impress me, so that made us close. And I latched on to him at a time when I needed a substitute maker, someone who *wanted* to teach me and value me."

At the reminder of what he had taken from her, Edward could feel her anger grow, even from across the room. The force of it made the hairs on his arms stand on end.

On the edges of his mind, he heard a whisper: *You took him from me just as I took your humanity from you.*

She had entered his head, catching him unawares, easing through him like a warm stream that bathed him inside and out. Impulsively, he reveled in the saturation, then blocked her out once he realized what was occurring.

He should have stopped her from entering much earlier, yet as soon as she had come into him, it had felt so right.

Gisele barely paused at his rejection. If there was anything he had learned about her so far, it was that adversity never kept her down for long.

She unfurled more of the exotic cloth, holding it against her torso as if it was the most interesting thing in the room.

In spite of himself, he could almost see the innocent human she had been: the young woman who had dreamed in cinema hues, the shine of a movie projector dancing in her eyes.

The part of Edward that longed for even a hint of his own mortality opened itself to the sight. Did she also wish for those days to return?

He shifted, hearing his chains protest.

The sound provided all the answer he required. Gisele put the *vamp* in *vampire*. She was clearly the type to embrace the decadence, the blood and fangs and darkness.

Yet, as she sighed, still holding the fabric to her, she peered around the attic and changed the subject to a less volatile one. "Such forgotten treasures. Such potential. What sort of people do you think lived here?"

Refusing to further engage with her, Edward forced himself to lean his head back and close his eyes, even as he heard her opening more chests, dragging heavy materials around, then pounding something into the wall. She did it all with preternatural speed, compressing an hour's work into minutes.

Somewhere along the line, he even caught the faint thump of a door closing downstairs. Edward was too weak to scent it, but he supposed that Sam had come home to tuck in before dawn arrived.

"There," she finally said.

Peeking through his lashes, he saw that she was standing in front of the big window. It was now shrouded in canvas, blocking out a sun that would be rising soon.

She grabbed the red-orange cloth and took it with her as she walked toward the door in the floor. "It would not do for you to burn to a crisp before we kiss and make up."

Her words sent an unwelcome thrill through his veins. Kissing on those breasts, over her skin, between her legs…

"If those are your plans for me," he muttered, "then by all means, uncover that window."

She ignored that. "Can I get you anything before I retire? Another blanket for comfort? Some blood for a nightcap? I have plenty, and I know you have been anxious to taste me."

He turned his face away, avoiding the crush of desire that threatened to squeeze the breath out of his chest in one, long, naked *Yesss.*

He heard her saunter across the floor, then dip something into the bath water and wring it out. The thud of a wet cloth sounded near his feet, and he knew that *she* knew about the semen—the infertile evidence of how he'd shared that orgasm with her.

And so much else….

Without a word, the moan of the door's hinges, then a bang, filled his ears, indicating that she had finally left him in furious silence.

Edward battled the ensuing army of *yes*es that screamed for her to come back.

THE FOLLOWING nightfall, Gisele stretched awake on the mattress she and Sam shared during their resting periods. As creator and created, they gravitated toward each other during the prone daylight hours, staying close. In fact, Gisele fed off the nearness of Sam because, since she had gifted him with her blood during the exchange, he, in essence, carried a part of her within him.

It drew her to him, just as it did with Edward.

She and Sam also liked to stay near each other in case of danger—a habit left over from being in the gang. To further ensure their safety, they had light-proofed the room, using materials found in the garage to hammer and seal wood and heavy cloth over the bedroom windows. Plus, they had set a number of booby traps around the house—wires that would trip primitive alarms, mainly—as a basic form of protection from intruders. However, since the property had such a mysterious history, they hoped local wariness would keep visitors away in the first place.

Sam arose at the same time as Gisele and, wordlessly, they went about preparing for the night. As always, they dwelled in darkness; not only did this house lack electricity, but they didn't need lights with their heightened vision, anyway.

And that was fine because light might attract the curious.

She fetched the gorgeous flame-and-sienna silk she had found in the trunk, then smoothed it over the mattress, running her palm over the cloth's sinful texture.

Again, she wondered who had lived here and left a treasure like this behind. Gisele began to concoct her own stories about the previous tenants: a traveling troupe of actors. An old maid who collected precious things but never wore them….

Her partner was gathering a new set of clothing to wear for tonight. A dark T-shirt and jeans. He undid the towel from around his waist, hardly minding that Gisele was in the room. They had lived around each other for decades and there was nothing sexual about their intimacy.

But if he had been Edward…?

A jag of hunger split Gisele, leaving a dull ache between her legs. Suddenly, she was all too cognizant of the modest nightdress she had found in one of the drawers and was wearing. The bathtub gown had been too damp to retire in comfortably.

Odd—she had not been so aware of herself in years. Yet after the way Edward had watched her touch herself last night, after the way she had heard his heartbeat banging for her and then entwining with the cadence of her own heart....

Gisele tried not to think about it, because there was something just below the surface of her musings that felt like an undertow, grabbing at her legs, yanking her until she could hardly stay afloat.

She just wished...

What? That someday the lust would turn deeper? That there would be an occasion when she would feel a more vital connection than she had ever known?

Vampires should not long for these things—not when they had so much already. Her good fortune should actually help her to forget how her mortal days had only been a bracelet of abandonment with all the free-love sex she had insisted she had wanted instead of something more substantial. But, even back then, she had known she was depriving herself, and the only time she had escaped the disappointment was in the cinema, where she felt life more keenly than anywhere else.

"Where did you go last night?" she asked Sam. "You were already resting when I came down here, so I couldn't ask."

"I didn't want to be around you and your guest, so I kicked around the countryside, looking for future feeding opportunities."

"Did you find any?"

Sam shrugged, and it captured Gisele's interest. He seemed too casual.

"Sammy," she said.

"What?"

He finished dressing, then grabbed his iPod and the laptop computer he traveled with. When they were near civilization, he always found a coffee shop or a spot where he could ride someone's wireless access to the wonderful world of cyber information and entertainment. Out here, it took more of an effort, but it had not yet stopped Sam from speeding around outside to discover a signal.

He continued. "I only found some girl near a bridge who wasn't afraid enough to be inside after midnight. Easy pickings if we don't go to the city tonight."

Gisele wondered who this girl was and why she made Sam look away while he talked. Normally, he did not mind sharing stories of his bites since they were like catnip to Gisele.

She filed all her questions away, her thoughts pulled toward Edward again. Always Edward. "You know I cannot go anywhere right now."

Did not *wish* to go anywhere.

"Ah, right. The chained-up smartmouth in the attic."

Gisele went to the bathroom and fished in a drawer for some scissors. When she came back, Sam fired off a query.

"So what are the plans for taming tonight? That is, unless you've already won over the wicked yet reformed gentleman bandit."

She shot her created a sarcastic glance and put the scissors to the silk, cutting off a proper length that would serve as a dress. As a vampire, Gisele had developed a sense for the latest fashion. In fact, she enjoyed the necessity of keeping up with the trends, just as Sam did with his computers.

"Wait, don't tell me," Sam said. "Edward was flip yet difficult."

"We made progress."

Sam headed out of the room to disable the traps as he did each waking evening, but her sensitive hearing had no problems picking up his voice. "Lost cause, Gisele. Pack it away. That's my opinion."

"Not yet." Gisele set about readying herself in the bathroom. "Being a newer vampire, Edward will need a meal soon, and I will be using that to show him just how wonderful a good drink can be. In fact, I plan to start winning him over with the drink of his life."

She twisted the silk here and there into a dress that tied behind her neck and brushed the middle of her thighs with soft caresses.

Feeling languid in this dress as well as in the thick summer-night air, she moved to the front door, where Sam was preparing to leave.

"I appreciate you giving me privacy," she said. "And I would very much like it if you would do me a favor, besides."

Sam narrowed his eyes, but that was only his way of asking what she needed.

"Please go to our kind neighbor just over the hill and bring him back," she finished.

"Gisele, you fed off Terrence Gorley last night, so you can't possibly need his blood."

She flashed an innocent smile.

"Blood for Edward," he said. "Okay, I get the plan."

He opened the door, but she stopped him before he could dash off to find a wireless signal.

"Give me an hour," she said. "I should be ready for Terrence at that time. Then you can scamper off to your little victim for the night."

"Any vampire worth his salt doesn't scamper. He skulks, Gisele."

And, with that, he was off in a blur of speed, stirring her hair before she shut the door and headed toward the attic. Tonight, Edward *was* going to come closer to accepting their bond.

After what she had in mind, he would not be able to resist.

WHEN EDWARD forced open his eyes, he found himself in a foreign place.

Actually, he was used to awakening in a different location most nights—going rogue and then hunting Gisele had required that. Yet he had fully expected to rise—and not shine—in the attic he had retired in last night.

But this?

This was a makeshift harem he barely recognized.

He pushed himself off of the floor, the clank of his chains loud in his ears. Around him, silk and satin draped the walls, meeting in the middle of the ceiling like an airy tent, in colors that reminded him of a long-ago sunrise. In addition, mounds of material doubled as a bed in the center of the room. Right above that, a few crystal strands from the chandelier sparkled in their new incarnation as a wind chime.

He thought he heard its notes grace the atmosphere, but the crystals weren't moving.

It was…laughter.

Her laughter. And it sparkled through him like all the hope he'd lost over the centuries.

Edward turned toward Gisele, his pulse catching in his throat.

Long-limbed and elegant in a sultry dress made out of the material she had found in the trunk last night, she leaned against the right-hand wall. Her hands were clasped behind her, making her breasts swell against the silk. She had slicked her shoulder-length black hair behind her ears and looked like a glamorous siren.

"My," she said, "aren't you a sleeper?"

He didn't point out that silver poisoning could probably account for that.

"Hungry now, Edward?" she asked.

"No. I'll eat once you're staked and I'm free."

"Without a meal, you won't survive that long."

A hint of wind huffed through the room, jostling the chimes and lifting Gisele's dress from her sleek thighs. As he forced his glance away, Edward belatedly realized that she had taken the tarp off the window, then opened one of the sections. Night creatures sang their dirges outside, mocking the increasing throb in his veins.

Why couldn't he control himself around her?

Determined to correct that, Edward stretched out his legs, realizing how sore he was from not moving around. His bare foot skimmed the cloth she had left him last night so he might clean himself, which he'd done, and he kicked the material away, rejecting the reminder of her so-called kindness.

Gisele pushed away from the wall and sauntered near, bringing the intoxicating scent of primal temptation with her. "I could unchain you from the wall and walk you around."

"Like a dog."

"It was only an idea."

She halted several steps away, and his gut tightened. Famished. So hungry….

He found himself pulling against his chains, just to get closer.

"I offered before," she said, "and I will offer again. Would you like to feed?"

Shaking his head, he tried to tell himself he could withstand this.

"Oh, Edward."

Gisele's gaze softened, as if she cared. He almost barked out a laugh at that.

"I do not wish for you to suffer," she said. "Truly. Why can we not be reasonable about our situation?"

"Because there's no reason in our world." His voice was warped by his appetite, by the fighting against it. "There's no middle ground."

"For a being who once sought exactly that, I cannot believe you would not even wish to explore the possibility."

She drew nearer, and her skin drove him red-hot mad.

At that moment, the door in the floor opened with a sighing groan, ushering in Sam and another man.

A human whose steady heartbeat spiked Edward's appetite until he couldn't restrain himself any longer.

5

THE INSTANT Terrence Gorley entered the attic, Gisele knew she had the advantage over Edward.

His eyes flared with a violent hunger she knew all too well, and she would have allowed herself a moment of triumph if not for the total lack of satisfaction that weighed on her.

Will it really matter if he breaks down and gives in to you right now? What good will this truly do?

The doubt kept nibbling at her. Yet this was how she was going to persuade the stubborn vampire to see reason, she told herself. This was a part of the taming that would keep her from having to kill him so she could carry on without fearing for her existence in the future.

She had started simply tonight by making Edward more comfortable, warming up the room and creating a bed—a reward—that would soon cushion him from the hard floor if he cooperated.

"Hello, Terrence," she said, modulating her voice to soothe the human while Sam stood just behind him. Her partner had obviously wheedled their neighbor here by swaying him, too, but it was Gisele's turn to take over.

She measured the enthralled man: broad of shoulder, thick in the arms—a specimen honed from the constant labor he invested in his land and horses. He even reminded her a bit of Gary Cooper with his blue eyes and golden hair, but her bite had given him a sexual glow he had been lacking before.

Bites did that to mortals, and Fegan had used their resulting susceptibility as questionable entertainment. Gisele tried not to remember times like that though: she would never admit that her former mentor had crossed boundaries that had made her uncomfortable; she preferred to remember the vampire who had sheltered her from the streets.

Behind Terrence, Sam took his leave, shutting the door as he aimed an are-you-happy-now? look at Gisele. He was going off on his own hunt for nightly blood.

With that mysterious girl by the bridge.

Gisele turned to Terrence, who still stood speechless, watching her as if she were all that existed. She knew from previously being in his head that he enjoyed giving his blood to her, enjoyed the carnality of being the submissive he never allowed himself to be with human women. This, too, would probably change because of her bite. She could imagine him using this newfound lack of sexual inhibitions to improve his life in many ways.

She looked to Edward, whose head was bent, his long, thick hair shielding his gaze as he pulled against his chains, panting. His blanket had fallen off his torso, baring the straining muscles of his chest and arms.

Her highwayman, she thought again. A dark yet smooth criminal who played to her most romantic night fantasies.

Her skin tingled, the vibration traveling lower, deeper.

"Since the notion of feeding from me appalls you," she said to him, "I have provided my own willing blood source. Terrence, our neighbor, has been very accommodating during my stay here."

"No." It sounded as if the refusal had been drilled out of Edward, his voice tight and tortured.

"You plan to shrivel away to a barely functional thing instead?" she asked. "That is hardly a brilliant scheme. They say that a lack of sustenance will only turn a vampire like you or me into a mindless, helpless entity who has withered from the inside out—a bloodthirsty being who becomes trapped in a body that does not work as it could. You cannot put an end to your own existence, Edward. We do not have that option."

His next words stirred the air with their force. "I don't plan to fade away. I only refuse anything you have to give."

The rejection stung. He was hers, and to be repelled was tantamount to having a vital organ fail.

"What do you suggest then?" she asked, containing her frustration. "Shall I unchain you so that you might hunt on your own tonight?"

Her facetiousness was not lost on him. She could see this in the amber eyes that glowed out from under his hair, a fierce gaze guaranteeing that she would be his only prey.

A driving roar of blood heated her up. The idea of being chased by him excited her, even though she knew the danger of it.

Something like a growl issued from his throat, and Gisele knew that it was only a matter of time until his orneriness abated and he gave in. She would have to push him to the point where he had no other choice— both for his health *and* their future.

She turned to Terrence, who had been waiting patiently, lavishing that adoring gaze on her the entire time. She had felt the press of his attention on her back.

"Are you ready?" she asked, sidling closer to the human.

He smiled, his eyes hazy with passion and anticipation. Terrence was a quiet, repressed man who was learning to let himself go, although at this point he could do it only when he was under a spell like hers.

"Good." As she moved next to him, his mortal aroma—musk and blood—clouded her senses. She nuzzled his warm neck, hearing his heartbeat kick at her temples and echo under her skin.

Blood, thick, delicious. But it would only be a dessert since she had eaten well the night before.

When her fangs emerged and her gaze had tinged to a crimson wash, she glanced at Edward, who was watching, in spite of his refusals, from under his hair. His own eyes flared.

His unwilling interest spurred her. It was not enough to make him want to drink for his health. Now she wished to stir a higher hunger within him.

She wanted Edward to need her as much as she did him.

Deliberately, she undid Terrence's denim shirt, one button at a time.

Another growl came from Edward's throat, this one lower, far more lethal. It settled into Gisele's belly, lubricating her into sweet agony.

"Ma chère," she said on a whisper, staring at Edward while slipping her hands over her prey's firm chest. His skin was warm, dewed with perspiration that gave a sensual complexity to his scent.

"Bite," she heard Terrence say under his breath.

His enthusiasm—not for her, but for what she could give him—stoked her hunger. Yet it was not Terrence's blood she wanted as much as Edward's devotion.

The realization surprised her. Did she want to tame him?

Or did she secretly wish that this vampire who seemed to match her heartbeat by heartbeat, craving by craving would accept her without having to be tamed?

The question lingered as she eased off the human's shirt. She heard Terrence's heart hammering against his chest, saw how his nipples tightened under her gaze. For Edward's benefit, she traced her tongue around one of those nubs, the salt and heat of the human's skin an aphrodisiac. His hands clutched at her shoulders.

This could be you, Edward, she thought, hoping he would allow her into his mind so he would see how much she craved him. *I could be your fantasy in the flesh instead of your enemy. We could fly so high together.*

And, when he surprisingly offered no resistance to allowing her into his head, Gisele's blood pumped all the harder.

EVEN AS her words rang in his addled mind, Edward couldn't deny how much he wished he were the one beneath Gisele's lips.

Battling his chains—but knowing that they were his only saviors right now—he allowed himself to be this other man who had thrown back his head in ecstasy.

Edward's red-lusted gaze tracked every shallow breath, every groan, becoming Terrence just for a moment. Just for a weak second.

As she took the man's other nipple into her mouth, Edward felt the tug on his own chest, felt the sexual current running through his limbs and straight to his cock. Then, when her neighbor repeated, "Bite," and pulled Gisele down to the harem bed she had created, Edward had to depend on the chains that bound him to hold him up.

It was happening again—the foreign connection of being wanted so badly by another.

But…how? Why was he unable to hold back?

Generally, vampires like him learned to cool their emotions and turn to superficial pleasures during such a long life; they had to because feelings could stay and grow—and hurt—for centuries. But with Gisele, it was as if all defenses had been peeled from him, leaving him emotionally raw.

At a gust of a warm breeze, the wind chimes came alive. Saliva ran hot and wild in his mouth, bathing his fangs. The silks and satins hovering over the bed undulated, waves of languid motion.

Maneuvering so that she faced him, Gisele straddled the other man, her silk dress fluttering, too, the hemline riding to the tops of her thighs. Edward's cock stiffened at the shadow just underneath her dress, between her legs, as she hovered over her prey's stomach.

"Do you not want this for yourself, Edward?" she asked. "You know the act of drinking is so much more than a meal. Or, in your denials of our kind's pleasures, have you reduced it to a numb chore?"

He flashed his fangs at her, warning her to back off.

But she was right—he drank, but only because he had to, and the process had become rote, even though the stimulation lingered, ready for the taking if he wished it. Back when he'd first been turned, he'd enjoyed it too much, and then he'd tempered the lust with intellectual pursuits that seemed so much profounder and…safer.

Had he repressed himself while pining for what he couldn't have—humanity?

Had he romanticized a lost mortality in the process?

A rustling inside his head told him that Gisele had

slipped in to read him again. She even seemed nourished by this new information he'd just provided to her *and* himself.

As if urged on, she leaned forward and ran one hand up her prey's chest, then to his throat. There, she moved her palm up and down, priming him. The human groaned, obviously knowing what was soon to come.

And Edward felt every stroke, just as if she were ready to drive in to *him*.

"What we vampires have," she said, "is beyond what any mortal could ever experience. You *did* cut yourself off from pleasure many years ago, Edward, and you have forgotten the bliss, the sublimity."

He couldn't accept that. He'd become unnatural, something to fear. His was an existence rife with depravity, and he could not stand to think of all the nights that lay ahead, choked with the hell of having to endure himself.

His longevity wasn't a gift—it was a curse.

"You prefer this intimacy to a purer one?" His voice was mangled. "Perhaps your sexual experiences as a human weren't all that gratifying."

He didn't add that perhaps he suffered from the same possibility.

She paused in her stroking, but only for an instant. When she resumed, she seemed to direct even more energy to her caresses.

"I was free with my attentions," she said, "just as many during the seventies were. Sex was a release. It felt…so very *good*. Most of the time. But it could feel so hollow, as well."

In spite of Edward's aroused state, something within his chest sank at that.

Before he could stop it, snaps of memory clicked

through his mind, and he felt Gisele there with him, watching the pictures, too: taking giggling village girls on a mound of hay in the stables. Thrusting in to a buxom server or two in the upstairs room of a public house. He had never fully invested himself in any of them, believing that one day, when he was ready to face his father, there would be high-station women who deserved all of him.

Had this lack of connection been the reason he had always searched for more?

Gisele slid through his head, reminding him she was still there. But she took him aback when she offered her own memories, as if giving up a little of herself, also.

She showed him a young blond biology student dressed in black who had romanced her in the midst of all her cinematic decadence. He'd pursued her with flowers, but when he'd caught her, the flowers had stopped coming. Then he had, as well.

She had tried again with another student. And another. Yet after several disappointments, she'd stopped expecting flowers. Stopped expecting anything....

Her memory touched the core of him, a blast of the emotion he'd tried so hard to quell. Instinctively, he blocked her, and his hunger returned full-force.

Empty, Edward thought. *So empty without her inside.*

"Bite," the neighbor said. "Give it over...."

In reaction to being kicked out of Edward's head, Gisele stared just a beat too long at him. Then, blinking slowly, as if acknowledging that this was how they would have to continue, she arched feline-like over Terrence.

The human rocked his hips, and Edward knew it was because the prey wanted more of her. And from the look on her face, Edward realized she would oblige him only because Edward had rejected her again.

A slow burn suffused him. All he could do was watch, crave…

She fitted her mouth next to the prey's ear, as if to whisper. But instead she gently yet forcefully bit his neck, bringing the human's groans to a crescendo as she sucked.

Edward squeezed shut his eyes, unable to take it.

Blood…sweet blood…her mouth kissing, sucking…

He pushed it all out, pushed and pushed.

And after what seemed like an excruciating hour, he heard her whispering to him.

"Edward?"

He moaned, deep in his chest.

"Edward, are you hungry *now?*"

His gaze flew open, his tolerance at an end. Blood. *Blood.* He smelled it on the air, even though she was pressing her hand to the man's neck in a healing touch.

"Even just a harmless sip?" she asked, her lips vivid with a darker crimson as she finished her ministrations and then primed the prey's arm.

Edward guessed what she might have in mind since he, the repressed vampire, wouldn't deign to feed at the neck in front of her. It was one of the most sexually provocative places for his kind, and she'd figured out that he would not give her the satisfaction of watching him.

"Please," the human said. "More."

She cradled the prey's arm and fixed her gaze on Edward again. His pulse was throttling him by now, flashing deep red over his eyesight.

"So delectable, this skin," she whispered. "And his blood, Edward. *His blood.*"

Gently, she used a nail to open her prey's wrist. The

overwhelming return of blood scent hit Edward's nostrils, flipping him inside out.

He raged against the chains, a madman with no ability to think anymore. All he could taste in the juices flooding his mouth was the promise of sustenance. The dizzy foreplay of it.

Need, Edward thought, the word becoming a stabbing pattern of anguish. *Need, need, need—*

But what he needed more than anything was her.

"Do you want it, Edward?" Gisele asked, and he knew just what his acquiescence would bring.

It would be a victory for her in this taming game, but he'd gone beyond caring now.

Need—need—need—

Reaching out his hands as far as they could get, he welcomed his next meal.

Neeed—

Gisele tenderly led the prey to Edward, then pressed his wrist to Edward's mouth.

Latching on to the human, Edward sucked greedily, using the prey as a substitute for what he really wanted as the new blood diluted the silver poison in his own body. He was so lost in feeding that it was only after the initial gluttony that he detected Gisele's touch on his head.

Her fingers stroked in rhythm to every draw of his mouth, and for the first time in years, feeding became more than an act of survival for him.

The combination of the blood and her touch was comfort incarnate. A night in the arms of someone who was there to hold him against the cold.

But as he took his fill, Edward grew stronger, and his mind sharpened.

Not her. He *didn't* need his enemy.

Having had enough, he backed away from the prey, backed away from Gisele's hand, which still remained outstretched, in contact with emptiness.

He sought the wall, which stiffened his back and girded his determination. A trickle of blood remained near his mouth, and he slipped out his tongue to lick the last of it while his gaze readjusted to the darkness and his fangs receded.

Meanwhile, Gisele was the one who seemed drained, perhaps because her barehanded contact had allowed the silver to get to her. Whatever the reason, her shoulders slumped as she tilted her head at him.

But then she stood, and he realized she was the one who had triumphed here, not him.

Yet she didn't lord it over him. Instead, she bent down and touched her prey's wrist to heal him, then rested her fingers against the man's forehead, willing him to rest and clearing his mind of this event.

Afterward, in what would seem like the blink of an eye to any human, she carried the slumped mortal to the door in the floor and disappeared with him.

Several minutes later, after Edward had stopped reeling, she returned with her arms empty.

"He's sleeping soundly in his bed now," she said, shutting the door behind her as she came to stand before Edward in that sanguine-swirled dress. "But for us, the night is only beginning."

Edward grinned, hoping his facade would still work on her. "I do hope you're stepping up your taming game then, because I'm no farther from resisting."

She smiled back, the gesture razor-edged.

AFTER SAM had motored out of the house, sans computer this time, he headed as far away as he could get.

He'd brought his iPod, so he sat on a large rock near a burbling creek on the property, waiting for midnight and listening to a Podcast from some fringe UFO group.

The conspiracy theories gave him a few jollies. However, all the while, his appetite grew, rumbling in his veins. He even thought of snatching up some woodland creature as a first course but thought better of it; based on the amazing aroma of the girl from last night, her blood was bound to match his tastes well, and he didn't want to spoil his appetite.

There were meals and then there were *meals*. Tonight he'd get the better of the two.

By the time he moseyed over to the bridge and scented her presence, he was famished.

He turned off his iPod when he found her sitting near the grass-quilted bank of the river under the bridge. She was wearing a dress similar to the one from last night, and the skirt draped over a pair of curvy thighs, the material flirting with the warm breeze. She'd left her curly dark hair to flow over her shoulders while she concentrated on twisting what looked to be strands of the long grass in her hands

For a time, Sam couldn't move. Somehow, he only wanted to keep watching her, just as his blood-brother Stephen had once watched his Savannah belle, Cassandra, below her window.

Stephen used to tell such tales of how he would go to the square where her home stood, how he would blend with the trees' shadows and take in the sight of her combing her hair out in front of the bedroom mirror.

The story hadn't ended well for Stephen and Cassandra, of course—human/vampire relations rarely did, and Sam was darn sure his former brother's new obses-sion with the mortal Kimberly was headed for a crash, too. Yeah, Stephen was human now, so the couple had that in common, but they had started out with him as a vampire, and it mattered.

It would always matter.

Sam drank in the girl as moonlight bathed the bridge above her in a deceptively serene blue. This was the closest he would ever get before the bite changed everything. This was the last time he would look at his leisure.

Why he wanted to dwell on her, he wasn't sure. It just seemed…right. It made him feel as if something solid had been poured into him, making him fuller than he'd ever expected to be.

In the midst of all this, she looked up, and Sam stood straighter. How had she known he was here?

"Hey!" she said, waving at him.

Sam jerked his chin at her and sauntered closer. Under the bridge, they would be hidden from the road enough to do what he needed to do in the still of the night.

His hunger gnawed at him from the veins out, but he focused on controlling his urges. Soothe her, then strike. That was the best way.

"I thought you might've found something better to do tonight," she said.

"What's better than this?" he asked, coming within a foot, then grinning at her.

The flutter of her eyelashes told him that his charm had hit its mark.

"I'll tell you what would be better," she said, gestur-ing to his earbuds.

"Oh." He'd forgotten the iPod was still hooked up to him. He spent so much time with his accessories that they seemed like limbs.

"Sorry about that," he said, taking the device off and stowing it in a pocket. He'd need his hands free.

She tucked a curl behind an ear, then patted a flat rock next to her. The moonlight had found an angle under the bridge, providing faint illumination.

He sat, still fighting the instinct to launch himself at her. But all he had to do was start to soothe her with his voice and he would soon have his meal.

So why wasn't he doing it?

His reluctance perplexed him. She was food. Blood was his life.

"You know," she said, "I'm not used to being in the dark with a stranger."

"We met last night."

"So that makes you a kind-of stranger. Big difference."

He didn't have the heart to tell her that strangers were all they'd ever be.

But why did he care that she might be seeing this as some sort of courtship? A strange courtship, to say the least, but he was getting that distinct feeling from the way she was looking at him so eyelashy and smiley.

Was she so lonely that she had come here just to be with someone else? He had a bad feeling that this was the reason she'd been meeting with the mortal man who was supposed to be here last night.

She was already sticking out her hand. "By the way, my name's Corinna. Corinna Smalley."

When he shook hands with her, he did it quickly, but not fast enough to halt a vibration that zinged from his fingers to his arm.

"I'm Sam," he said, detaching, then planting his free hand on a bent knee, trying to look casual. Sure.

Besides a brief glance at his hand, she didn't comment. "Cold hands on such a warm night?"

"Cold-blooded." He laughed.

She did, too. "How are things going at your cousin's?"

"All right." This small talk was getting to him—he should be halfway to paradise by now. "Who knows how long I'll be staying though. My cousin doesn't have a TV and there's not much else to do around here, so I might be off to another relative's place for the rest of the summer."

"Only a city boy would need a TV."

He could tell she was trying not to react to the news of him possibly leaving so soon, and the fact that he'd discouraged any romantic hopes in her was a relief. Wasn't it?

Something about the way they were sitting here reminded him of what it had been like nearly a hundred years ago, when he was just a kid in puppy love with Molly, who could pick a pocket on the street just as deftly as he could.

Sam turned away from that recollection. He had no ties to mortality—not like some of his former brothers.

Corinna went back to working the long strands of grass together, slowly, delicately. The activity seemed to fit with her fey nature, and so did the way she airily presented her next comments.

"I have a confession to make." Wide-eyed, she smiled at him, and the sweetness of it just about knocked him to his back. "You kind of remind me of an old boyfriend."

There it was: the reason she wasn't hauling butt away from a stranger in the dark.

"Maybe the moonlight isn't giving you the best view," he said, thinking it was time to enthrall her with his voice.

He'd do it in a minute. Really.

"No, you actually do resemble him," she said. "But we haven't been together for, oh, about five years now. You just…remind me."

He was tempted to peek into her head, but it seemed like an invasion, even if it never had been before with prey. Mind play was part of his existence, yet there was something about this girl that made him…well, respectful.

Sway her, his appetite whispered. *Her blood's waiting.*

But she was already talking, and he thought it might be impolite to interrupt.

"His name's Brian," she said, focusing on twisting those grass strands. It was almost as though she thought he wouldn't notice the hurt in her tone if she didn't look at him right now. "He was my high-school sweetheart until he found someone else when he went off to college. I thought it was a passing thing for him but… Heck, they got married a couple of years ago." She laughed, but she didn't sound happy. "How about that? I kept my candle burning bright for him and he was off saying vows to another woman and then had a baby with her just three months ago. Then he came back here, to his home, to make his parents proud with his sparkling new family."

This time, Sam did risk skimming the surface of her mind, so gently she probably wouldn't be able to feel it.

He found someone special, he heard her think. *Wasn't I special enough?*

When Corinna raised her head, looked around and frowned, Sam pulled away, knowing she'd detected something.

She was ultrasensitive, this girl.

He bit down on his pulsating thirst, telling himself that if he tried to use his sway on her again, she might become aware of it. Maybe she was even one of the few humans able to resist it. Rumor said they were out there, and Sam didn't want to chance tangling with one of them.

But he had sensed a need within her. A yearning to be valued for the unique qualities she hadn't yet found within herself. And a fear that it would never happen.

At that, he knew for certain it was time to cast his net in other waters. Too much trouble here.

He stretched his arms in a preamble to the wow-I-should-really-get-home excuse he was about to make, yet when Corinna flashed those big dark eyes at him— *Are you leaving already?*—he found that he couldn't carry through.

Great. And *he* was the one who was supposed to be swaying her. Where was his fierce survival instinct now?

When he didn't make a move to go, she smiled at him, and the area around his heart seemed to melt. He brushed a hand over it in disbelief.

"Old boyfriends," she said, her voice going into its dreamy cadence again. "Boring subject. Let's change it."

She held out the overgrown, twisted grass to him, keeping it intact by grasping both ends. "Tie this on me?"

Sam cocked his head at her.

"It's just a bracelet, not a ball and chain." She laughed and held it out to him again. "Come on."

When he took it from her, their fingers made contact, and his sight went red.

No—beat it back, beat it back….

Quickly—probably too quickly for the human he was supposed to be imitating—he secured the ends around one of her wrists then stood, already on his way down the hill toward the woods, his gaze clouded with crimson splashes, his gums aching with the pierce of his fangs.

"Sam?" he heard her say, a thin line of hurt striking through her voice.

He raised his hand in goodbye, not daring to look back.

Because if he did, he'd no doubt pay a price no smart con—or vampire—could afford.

6

GISELE STOOD before Edward in the attic, the night breeze at her back as they faced off.

She had summoned her fangs only to intimidate him and not because of hunger—although she was not far from that. After she had put Terrence to bed in his home, she had known that the moment she stepped foot in front of Edward again, there would be a battle.

She leaned down to whip the blanket away from around his shoulders. The act left him bare-chested, garbed only in his trousers, which sported a darkened spot on the material near his groin, evidence of the simultaneous orgasm he had enjoyed with her during last night's bath.

The stain made her go soft for a moment because, more than anything else, it revealed what he was denying.

As if detecting her weakness, he glanced up at her and bent one knee, resting an arm upon it, as careless as could be.

"Your trousers," she said, taking neutral ground. "It seems they need a more thorough cleansing after what we put them through."

"Why, Gisele—without a blanket or a stitch of clothing, I'm sure to catch my death in this breeze coming through the window."

"Do not be disingenuous," she said. Time to be straightforward. "Shall I remove your pants or shall you?"

He stared at her, his calm amber gaze belying a jerk of blood in his veins that she caught just below the humming air. She did not break their linked glares, would not back down as the atmosphere grew so brittle it all but cracked.

One second, two… Neither of them even blinked. The throb of her clit sharpened to agony.

As if knowing that, a mirthless smile tilted Edward's lips. He could probably scent her arousal, feel it in his very marrow.

He unbuttoned the top of his trousers, and she realized he was only doing it because removing the rest of his clothing might put her at a greater disadvantage than it would him.

Her mounting desire proved that theory correct.

"I've heard how powerful your will can be," Edward said, his voice low as he began unzipping his fly.

The buzz of it tickled her eardrums, then vibrated down her body in a delicious shiver.

Swallowing, Gisele imagined that Edward had done every bit of possible research on her, including chatting with all his humanized blood brothers—her former vampire gang mates. They would have told him her habits, her strengths and weaknesses, and her captive was even now using those to hunt her, although he was the one chained to a wall.

"I suppose you picked Stephen's brain clean for information about me," she said.

"I would've been a fool not to."

He paused halfway down his fly, teasing her with the sight of a patch of hair that trailed from below his navel.

As Gisele imagined what came next, her red vision beat like a wayward pulse, engaging her heart, which she had always considered useless.

But not now. Not whenever she was with Edward.

"I am sure," she said, "your friends provided you with enough of my background for you to realize that I will not surrender once I set my mind on a goal."

"That's obvious from how you wiggled into the gang. And I heard about how you used to research marks, then seduce them with your wiles while the boys made off with the riches of the household. No matter how long it took to reel in your mark, you always followed through."

He sounded surprisingly impressed with her tenacity, and narrowed his eyes, as if tempted to venture into her mind in order to glimpse one of these seductions. But he did not. Doing so would be a sign of voluntary connection, a concession for him, and they both knew it.

"The gang also told me that your true maker abandoned you after turning you in an empty, darkened theater," he added, as if, in one final effort to remain cool, he would put her worst memory between them instead. "He healed all physical evidence of the exchange and then just left you to fend for yourself."

His words cut into her, but she could have sworn that something like sympathy had come to shade his gaze in the aftermath.

Or was it empathy, because he knew what it was like to be betrayed by a creator?

Neither of them spoke as the moment folded into itself, bridging them…until even that collapsed when Edward went cool again—the distant gentleman.

Half of her wanted to tell Edward how much she regretted re-turning him, but the other half fiercely clung to the hope she had of redeeming herself by making him as ecstatic as she knew he could be in this existence— a happiness he had never found before.

She only wished he would participate of his own free will.

His next question was softer, utterly genuine, but still light years away from where she wanted him.

"Why have you never tracked your maker down to serve him justice?"

She shook her head, suspecting he had only asked out of curiosity as to how killing her maker might free *him*.

"Why are you so concerned?" she asked. "Unless you have come across evidence that killing my own master would make both of us mortal."

"As far as I know, that's not how it works. Only you would get the benefit of a soul."

Gisele considered his question. Why *hadn't* she tracked down her maker? Simple. "He has not presented a threat to my physical existence. But I used to think of finding him, just as you found me. Yet…"

Leaning away from the wall, Edward did not allow her thought to die. "Yet what?"

Finally, her mind coalesced. "I like what I am. Whether he intended it or not, he gave me something that I turned into a gift."

"I think you merely don't want to meet up with him again and chance another abandonment," he said.

She averted her gaze, his comment hurting more than she would ever show.

She would never again be the newly born vampire girl who had been deserted in that theater, the daughter who had been thrown out of the family apartment by her confused parents.

Grasping Edward's trousers, she tugged, as a reminder that he needed to finish doffing his clothing, then settled back into an aggressive crouch.

A stiff mockery of a smile weighed Edward's lips as he unzipped the rest of his fly.

Unable to stand another second of waiting, Gisele ripped his trousers the rest of the way off, tossing the material across the room in her fervor. Every inch of her was on fire, driving her mad.

She took a moment to comb a famished gaze over him: the muscled arms and chest. The ridged abs. The semi-erect state of his penis, thick and veined—

A pang of desire shook her, and she tore off her tied silk dress, leaving herself just as bare, the breeze dancing over her flesh. Her knees were parted, leaving her clit to beat with tiny explosions, her sex to go even wetter.

As she restlessly used both hands to push her hair back from her face, then ran her palms down over her neck, her chest, Edward's gaze roamed her, leaving a sizzling path wherever it traveled.

She approached without a thought to the danger, one meter, another. He tracked her with his gaze, his body taut against the chains.

Oh, his fragrance—a jungle scent that pounded against her, inside her…

All she wished to do was taste him, roll him under and over her tongue like a fiery liquor. He was hers, and she would prove their potency if he would just allow them to mix body and what they had left of their souls.

She grabbed her silk dress and made certain her hands were covered.

"I only want to make you feel good," she whispered. "Let me do that."

He kept watching, almost as if he understood that she truly did not intend any harm—only delight. She could make every mistake up to him, could make it all right if he would only let her.

Seizing this non-combative moment, she carefully reached her silk-covered hands out to part his legs. Edward hissed in a breath, leaning back against the wall.

"Even though I was on the run from you," she said, skimming her silken hands over his calves, his knees, his inner thighs, "I thought of you so often."

When she brushed the silk over the middle of his legs, his cock stirred, the tip dewing with come that, although sterile in the most basic way, would be warm and pungent in her mouth.

She used both hands to make a sling out of the dress, then captured his penis in its cradle. His arms pulled against the wall-bound chains, his hands fisting.

Encouraged, she worked the silk from side to side, rubbing the underside of his penis, rolling it as he arched his hips. He was getting hard, and all she craved was to work him into her mouth and lavish him with her tongue, then take him long and deep. With their connection, satisfying *him* would satisfy *her.*

Yet there was still the silver in his system… What effect would it have on her?

Almost beyond a care, she decided to take the chance of finding out. Somehow, making him happy seemed like the most important thing.

"Your skin is sensitized to the point of pain, isn't it?" she asked. "You know your responses could never be as pleasurable if you were mortal."

He bucked, and she deftly maneuvered the silk behind him, so she was holding one end in front and the other in back. Then she slid the material back and forth so it massaged his balls and another sensitive spot or two. He hitched in a breath, his fangs springing to full length, inspiring an answering arousal in her, too.

"And if you drank from me while we pressed skin to skin," she added, "you would come as you have never come before."

She could not keep her gaze off his engorged cock. The throb of him—the sound and scent of all the blood pooled there—debilitated her thinking.

Her own fangs scratched against her bottom lip as they thrust outward.

He opened his eyes, showing how they burned with hatred, but she wondered if perhaps he really hated himself more than the vampire he had become.

There were ways to find out.

She slipped the material out from between his legs and readjusted the ends of the silk around her hands, then rested them on top of his thighs, spreading his legs wider while allowing the material to drape under his erection to lift it at the base. Heedlessly, she lowered her mouth to him, just for a taste.

Just one.

As her lips made contact with his tip, he grunted, the pulling of his chains telling her that she had shocked him raw.

But her head was already swimming.

Silver poisoning? Yes, but the effects were faint, reminding her of a bitter essence barely disguised by layers of sweetness and cream. She was more weakened by the influx of him: the pain she wished to erase from his past.

Taking care with her fangs, she licked him up and

down, delighting in his thick length, relishing the beaded moisture on his head.

And while loving him so thoroughly, his defenses shattered, allowing her to edge into his mind.

What she saw there surprised her: utter chaos and ecstasy. Edward had not had sex *and* bitten a woman at the same time for over two hundred years.

He had been afraid to indulge, fearful that pairing sex with a bite would mean giving up his last traces of humanity.

Oh, Edward…

Driven by the extent of his sacrifice, she swirled her tongue around him as she moved up and down, minding her fangs. Her temples began to pound, her limbs feeling heavier, weaker.

She should really stop—

But she couldn't. No, she wanted this to go on and on because she feared she would never feel this way again: overjoyed, overcome, intimate in both body and mind.

When she paused to catch her breath, he thrust his hips, fighting to an erupting climax. At the same time, he cursed her, clawing at the air as the chains held him, and growling as if fighting her…

Fighting himself.

Releasing the silk and backing away from him— weak, oh, she felt so weak, but in such a wonderful way—she felt their link buckle under the orgasmic weight, felt him reach his peak as his juices soaked his thighs.

Coming to her part of their shared orgasm, she arched, biting her lip, going dizzy as her mouth flooded with her own saliva, her breathing short and harsh.

Then, on all fours, she glimpsed him through the

cover of her hair. What if she touched him—his cheek, his jaw? She dearly wished she could.

Yet she also wanted more.

His blood. A bite that would bring them crashing together in an even bigger climax.

The frenzy in his gaze told her he wanted it, too, but she also sensed that he would rather suffer the pain of hunger than allow them the pleasure.

She wiped a finger under her bottom lip, catching the last of him. "Edward…"

He started to shake his head, but was too sapped of strength, so he merely hung against his chains, trying to steady his breathing.

"I can give you blood, Edward."

"No," he whispered.

In spite of her better sense, she dipped into his mind. He was telling himself that, no matter how much he was trembling for it, her bite would remind him of the night he had lost what he thought to be everything.

But… She trembled with a different idea.

What if she offered to level the field?

What if she allowed him to bite *her?* Would that make him see that she was not out to repeat the mistake she had made?

But she knew he would not allow even that. Not yet.

"I assume that this was the capper for our night?" he finally said after their breathing had smoothed.

How could he be so removed from what had just occurred?

Instead of asking, she nodded, leaving Edward to himself to go downstairs, her progress shaky from the poisoning. Once in her bedroom, she donned a slim white dress she had found in a closet—a creation that looked as if a woman who dreamed of someday escaping to the city had stuffed it away during the 1970s—then left the house to travel less than one hundred yards to their neighbor's.

After checking on Terrence Gorley in his bed—and drinking just enough of his blood to cleanse the silver taint out of her—she nursed him, feeding him a leftover hunk of roast beef from his refrigerator, plus orange juice. She had done the same earlier in the night when she had put him to rest so he would regain strength.

Then she collected some of the human's newspapers and brought them back to her hideout, where she had something else in mind for the next phase of Edward's taming.

ALTHOUGH Gisele was gone, Edward hadn't fallen to rest.

He was too worked up.

His breathing quickened as the memory of her hands, her mouth sketched over his body. After the first few years of giving in to the indulgences of vampirism, he'd spent a long, long time shedding his blood instincts and refusing to revel in them. So he'd forgotten.

Forgotten the heights he could scale, forgotten the depths he could hit.

Experiencing them tonight had reminded him that he could become a thing like Fegan…or maybe even like his human father: a self-involved, unapologetic ass who had taken great satisfaction in gluttony and excess. Unfortunately, blood was not the only sustenance derived from a bite; Edward pulled sexual power from it, too, so sipping from a blood-bank packet or drinking from an animal had never satisfied him for more than a short time.

However, survival or not, every time Edward robbed

a victim of blood meant he moved a step toward that point of no return and away from a state of grace.

And he had *really* put some distance between him and that state tonight.

Regretful rage burned low in his belly, like a flame that never went out. When he thought of Gisele kissing and caressing him, the anger stoked him as he had never been stoked before.

Why her? he thought.

Soon, he heard a disturbance down below. Gisele? Or Sam? Without these silver chains his senses might've detected an identity.

Still, he hoped it would be Sam since Edward would've preferred his former gang member's derision instead of his captor's attentions.

Soon enough he had his answer when Gisele came through the door, and he tried to tell himself he was not happy with the outcome.

He tried very hard.

While she thumped a bundle of newspapers onto the makeshift bed, he took in the sleeveless cigarette-slim dress she was wearing. It occurred to him that he preferred her without clothing.

Defending against those thoughts, he decided to show her that he was entirely comfortable the way she'd left him, stripped and supposedly vulnerable. But when she swept a saucy glance over his nakedness, he wondered if his tactic was all that effective.

She retrieved one of the newspaper sections from the floor and brought it over to him. When he failed to take it, she set the reading material over his lap.

"I thought you might like some brain food," she said.

He didn't remark on how her graceful, feline movements testified to a recovery from the slight silver poisoning he'd noted before she'd left. Instead, he glanced at the paper's headlines.

Corruption in politics. Violence.

"Yes," he said, "humans are not as perfect as we are. Or perhaps I have that turned around?"

She shrugged, but he knew full well that Gisele had insinuated herself inside his head during their physical bout, nestling into him until he'd allowed her to witness a couple of fleeting doubts regarding the quest for his humanity. Of course she was going to pounce on that, no matter how negligible those thoughts had been.

"I have heard quite a few tales about you," she said, sauntering over to the pile of papers and picking up another one. "For instance, back when you were a country boy, you dreamed of introducing yourself to your noble-born father; you even took pains to improve yourself in anticipation of the grand day. But your dream never quite happened, so then you willingly became a highwayman and vampire, most likely because you thought *that* would be better than living as a cast-off wrong-side-of-the-blankets child for the rest of your days. Correct me if I'm wrong, Edward, but did your grass-is-greener outlook start long before you became a vampire seeking his soul?"

He withstood the sting of her observation, staring at her, daring her to go on and see how much he could take.

Unruffled, she asked, "I wonder… Why did you go ahead and agree to vampirism before you had worked up the courage to confront your own father?"

He wouldn't allow her to get to him. "My mother was sickly, and she passed on, and I realized that I had only wanted to meet the man who sired me for her sake." That's what he had believed, anyway. "Then Fegan recruited me. At first my interest in meeting my father was revived because I believed that I could use my new abilities to impress my way into his acceptance. But it didn't take me long to realize I had overestimated my new lot in life."

"Or was it because your father might have turned you away, and you could not bear the possibility, so you never even tried?"

"*You* tell *me* about abandonment," he suggested.

In spite of his civil tone, she flinched, holding his gaze. Then, as if rethinking her strategy, she tossed the paper she'd been holding.

He did away with his own section, too, as she eased over to the other side of the attic to stare out the window. Then, as if she'd hit upon yet another idea to tame him, she shut the window and shrouded it with the heavy draping. Sunrise couldn't be more than a few hours away—he felt it stalking the air, just as he felt a niggle pulling at the fringes of his own consciousness.

There was a danger in him taunting another about being alone. After leaving the gang, Edward had combed the world for meaning, weaving in and out of other clans and exploring their cultures, then leaving before he became too much a part of the fabric of their lives. Could it be that he had missed connecting with others on a more profound level both as a vampire *and* as a human?

By this time, Gisele had turned around, her posture confident once again. There was no defeat that lasted with her, and Edward couldn't help but admire that a little.

"When was the last time you flew, Edward?" There was a glimmer in her light-brown eyes.

He found himself enthralled by that sparkle in her

gaze. It seemed to light into the center of him, as well, and he had never felt such a sensation.

Why would it happen now though? With *her?*

Because she was his maker?

Edward wasn't entirely certain anymore.

She continued. "I am not speaking of transporting yourself from one place to another through the air. I am asking when you *really* flew?"

"I've flown out of necessity quite often, especially while on your trail."

"Out of necessity." She took a step away from the window. "How about flying through the night for no reason at all? Or maybe only to shimmy up to the heights of a building or a hill to see the lights from a city and think about what grand adventures might await you there?"

Hah—she was playing him, and even with a nudge of excitement in his belly, he resisted.

"My," she said. "You truly are more stubborn than a donkey."

But she seemed in a chipper mood as she wandered over to the trunk, where her gloves rested on top. After donning them, she lifted the lid and brought out a folded mound of clothing, including a long jacket that she secured around her.

Before he knew it, she had zipped across the room, and he was dressed in baggy old jeans and an equally battered shirt, standing off-balance on his feet because she had also undone the chains from the wall moorings. He was still bound by the silver wrapped around his throat and wrists.

Before he could sink to his knees from silvered weakness, she took him by the wrist and swept him into a whir of motion, and they were downstairs, through the door, then outside, cutting through the air as she flew them both through the skies.

At first, it was like every other here-to-there flight, but then Gisele spiraled so that he was looking down at the moonlight-bathed hills.

Before, he'd always been wrapped in a destination, a purpose. Yet now that he had caught up with Gisele, he had nowhere else to go.

Almost in spite of himself, he finally looked past his anger and down at the blades of grass bleeding together into a sea of deep green.

A green that...

He blinked.

Dazzled.

As Gisele set them upright, she entered his mind. *Mortals have invented devices to do this. Airplanes. Spacecraft. They even have caped heroes who play out this dream for them.*

For a moment, Edward gave himself over to the weightless flaunting of gravity that their kind used to hunt and travel short distances. Just for a minute, and then he would think of how to escape her.

After all, he had already fallen so far...

He dipped down, yet Gisele held tightly to him, guiding him to the rooftop of a high building that boasted a pole flashing a red light. They came to a walking landing there, and she led him to the ledge, where they overlooked those city sparkles she had talked of before.

The lights twinkled at him, just like candles guttering out.

She noticed how he'd been peering at the city. "We

can feel in a way that they cannot. Their perception is dull, the hues of their surroundings lacking our color. Or do you not *want* to feel that keenly, Edward? Is that the reason you would rather be human—because every sensation is not as sharp as it is now?"

Her comment, an echo of all those nights of listening to his newly human brothers attempting to talk sense into him, scrambled all the sureties that had always existed for Edward.

He felt the weight of Gisele's presence in his mind, and his first instinct was to cuff her out. Yet, he refrained this time. Maybe if she understood, she would back off. She would realize he was a lost cause, unchangeable, and then drop this entire game.

But where would that leave them?

The odd question unsettled Edward but, in the end, there was one thing he was sure of: he could not be in a world that tolerated Gisele's unpunished presence.

When she withdrew, he relaxed, thinking he had won just this tiny battle.

Even if it seemed like an empty victory.

Exhausted, he lowered to a crouch, still on guard. If he were a wise creature, he would build his strength so he could eventually strike out at her and end this exercise in futility.

Gisele turned away from the city lights and stared at the opposite view, where darkness reigned. "I understand you, more than you even realize. If you could only admit how alike we really are, we could be such a comfort to each other, creator to created."

"This is only about mastery for you?"

"It's about—" She pressed her lips together, fixing her gaze on the blackness. "It's about what you said before, I suppose. Having someone stay when all they ever seem to do is leave."

Her forthrightness stunned him and, in the resulting silence, the lights of the city burned into a night that felt more fathomless than ever to him.

7

ABOUT an hour before dawn, Sam decided he should get on home.

He had already taken his time feeding on a wild turkey he'd found roaming the woods, thinking that this prey was way less nutritious, yet way safer than Corinna.

But why even think about her any more when sunrise was on its way?

He sped back to the house, thinking of her nonetheless. It was as if he'd run through a spiderweb and couldn't brush the silk off his skin.

He was distracted, all right, but he managed to enter the hideout quietly in time to see Gisele coming down the attic stairs. She was wearing some mod white dress she'd obviously dug up around this old place but, somehow, Gisele made it look cutting edge with her svelte figure and hip hair.

"How was tonight's folly?" he asked while heading toward the bedroom. He couldn't wait for the blankness of rest.

"A work in progress." She smiled, but Sam didn't detect much satisfaction in the gesture.

Once in the bedroom, he plopped onto the mattress, not even bothering to remove his clothing. The sooner he could go dark, the better.

Still, images of Corinna, with her gypsy hair and fresh summer dress, haunted the backs of his eyelids when he closed them.

But why? Possible prey had never affected him like this. Did it have something to do with chemistry, like a certain food one loved to eat more than all the others?

"Sam?" Gisele said, standing by the bed.

He grunted as a substitute for "What?"

His creator sighed, and he opened one eye to a slit, finding her fidgeting with the seam of her dress.

"I'm going to guess that I won't like what you have to say," he muttered.

"Probably not." She gestured in the direction of the attic. "Edward has improved somewhat, and I am thinking of relocating him to a more comfortable place."

"Where? Out of our hair?"

Gisele sighed. "Actually, I would like to give him a sense of freedom in return for his better attitude. I can use the canvas in the garage for a tent of sorts outside. It would block the sun while Terrence kept watch during the day."

Sam laughed. Gisele was on some Rudolph Valentino kick now. This whole taming was going too far.

"I would at least like to spend the night near him," she added. "He is coming around."

A torrent of alienation made Sam's chest feel as if it were sinking into itself, and he opened his gaze all the way. "You're playing right into his hands."

"Hardly."

"I'm serious, Gisele. At first, you were across the room from him. Then I'll wager you got even closer while he was chained to the wall. Now there're no walls at all. Believe me, I spent years with this guy, so I know he's not stupid. He was always the shadow in every robbery, the one who was quiet but effective."

"He is coming around. I have seen into his mind, but you have not had that luxury."

Sam noted how her heartbeat got louder at the mention of being inside Edward's mind. And if he looked at her more closely, he could even see the pulse of blood under her skin, beating and rushing.

"You're attached to him," he said. "He's wrapped you around his finger."

Gisele opened her mouth to deny it, but Sam interrupted.

"I don't forgive him, and you shouldn't, either."

"Please, have some faith in me."

Didn't she see what was happening? For the first time, she slipped a bit from the pedestal Sam had put her on. She'd been his second savior, but what was he supposed to think now?

"You'd best not forgive," he said, "because Edward Marburn will take every inch you give him and turn it into a mile."

"Sam…"

He closed his eyes again, but instead of entering a restful state, he felt the beginning of a profound isolation.

He heard her hesitate to leave him, but then she finally shut the door and climbed the stairs back up to the attic. Maybe, up there, she'd rethink rewarding Edward with a tent that would only make escape easier.

He heard the attic door open, then close, and he wondered if his anger actually hid some envy. For the past two years, Gisele had belonged to *him,* but now Edward was in the picture, threatening the existence Sam had reclaimed.

He stilled his mind, huddling into himself until blackness swallowed him. And when he next awakened, it was to a bed that was as empty as it'd been last dawn.

The sense of isolation returned full force, devouring him. He hated this: it reminded him of the awful time after his human brother had died and left him to fend for himself on the streets at a young age.

Now he was alone again.

Would he always end up this way?

Sam wouldn't accept that. Why should he when he had the ability to get just about anything he wanted?

Without even checking in with Gisele—he couldn't stand the thought of seeing her with Edward—Sam readied himself, changed into another pair of jeans and another dark T-shirt, then greeted the night outside. She would know that he was hunting.

His anger led him to the woods near the bridge, but he knew he was just fooling himself. He wanted to see if Corinna was around, because he was just frustrated enough to do a dumb thing like sink his fangs into her.

Even the anticipation of her flavor assuaged him, and he calmed his breathing, coming to the edge of the woods so he could see the bridge.

It was too early for her to be there, so, banning all reason, Sam threw his concentration into tracking her.

He sniffed the air, thought of her cocoa skin, the rounded curves under her dress….

When he caught a hint of her on the night, he followed, speeding past the bridge up a hill to a graveled road whose trees hid small, dilapidated houses with tin siding. Light glowed in the windows, and Sam moved closer, Corinna's essence growing stronger, sweeter….

In the near distance, he slowed down, hearing voices—a man and…Corinna?—and then the slam of a car door. The purr of an engine. Gravel spitting out from under tires as the vehicle took off.

He'd bet anything it was her.

Sam halted at the side of the lane just as a 1976 mint-green Dodge Aspen took a curve at a mad clip. The headlights glared while the vehicle bore down on him.

Look at me, he thought, reaching out with his mind, not caring how obvious the trickery might be to Corinna.

The car flew past him, then braked to a stop that stirred up a cloud of dirt. The taillights bathed the pines near the road in red, encouraging Sam to contain his hunger, lest the driver see it and speed away.

He could discern a riot of wild hair as she glanced in the rearview mirror.

Corinna, he thought, his chest beginning to ache as she temporarily soothed his sense of alienation.

She backed the car up, then came to an equally abrupt halt in front of him, her window rolled down.

Her dark eyes were wide, surprised. "Sam?"

He stood, waiting to be invited in. Willing it without actually entering her mind again.

She seemed to be on the same wavelength as she re-checked her rearview mirror, then waved him over. "Well, what are you waiting for?"

There. So easy.

He climbed into the passenger seat, the white vinyl clean and smooth. He belted up.

The second he was settled, she took off, zooming down the lane, the rocks and foliage rustling. He saw that she was wearing that grass bracelet he'd put on her wrist last night, although it'd gone slightly dry.

"You're a real restless guy at night, aren't you?" she asked, peering in that rearview mirror again.

He avoided her fishing for information. "Are you nervous about something?"

"How can you tell? Is it because I flew down the lane like a bat out of…"

Sam steeled himself for the H-word that might cause wracking discomfort.

But when she ended with *heck,* he laughed to himself. It helped him to deal with the grumbling in his core, the need exacerbated just by being around her.

"Maybe I shouldn't tell you," she said.

"I'll end up finding out."

An odd look settled on her features.

"Kidding," he said, telling himself to cool it.

She blinked, unguarded once again. "I did a bad thing, Sam. Promise you won't hate me for it."

"What could *you* do that's so bad?"

Her smile, so innocent, went off-kilter. "I don't know *what* I'm doing anymore. You'd think a girl would be over an old relationship. Right? But I've been doing things I'd never have done before Brian the ex came back to town with his wife and baby."

Wasn't I special enough? she had thought after telling him about the old boyfriend who'd deserted her.

"You're at an age when you're discovering yourself," he said. "That's not so strange."

Corinna stopped the car at the end of the lane, by a lonely highway stretching along the country hills. "Wow, that was sage. How old are you? Like, seventy?"

He realized his error. "Twenty-five," he lied, thinking he could get away with it.

Clearly, it was beyond him to act normally around her, so he'd have to watch himself if he wanted to…

Do what? It was too late to bite and run.

Smart, Sam, he told himself. *You're just setting yourself up for discovery.*

As she took the highway and then a sharp turn down another lane, she continued. "Anyway, what I've been doing lately is strange, at least for me. I've been taking these…risks. It's like I don't care about what happens, either."

"So what did you do tonight?"

"Oh, tonight." Her feyness shone through now. "I was just coming from this fellow named Ned's place. I met him at the grocery store about a month ago, and we've been meeting by that bridge most nights. My friends think I can do better than him, so I've been secretive about the whole thing, meeting him late and going off with him in his car for an hour or two so we can…"

Sam turned to look out the window.

Corinna laughed. "All we did was kiss a little. Talk. You know."

Still. "Why did he agree to meet you so late?"

He could feel the heat from her blushing.

"He's living with someone." She turned another corner. "But he told me they broke up. She just hadn't moved out yet, and he wanted to wait until she did before we went public. That's what he said, anyway."

"They haven't broken up," he said, because he knew how this story was going to end.

"I found out the big news tonight." Her mortification permeated the air.

Sam wanted to tell her that she deserved more than being strung along by a scallywag.

"So how did this guy manage to hook you in?" he asked.

She paused. "He's funny. Charming as all get out. But…"

"He's not Brian the ex?"

Corinna smiled at Sam, as if relieved that he got it.

"I've been thinking a lot about this since the other night—when Ned didn't show up to meet me—and I've come to a conclusion." She straightened her arms as she gripped the wheel in an odd shrug. "I haven't dated anyone seriously since Brian, but since he's come home, something inside me wanted to prove that he doesn't have a hold on me anymore. So I went to the extreme by meeting Ned at night and sneaking around, doing stuff I usually wouldn't do."

So that explained her openness to Sam by the bridge. Extreme chances.

As he thought about this guy she'd been meeting, something like jealousy pressed at him again. Maybe that came from his old habits though: hoarding what little food he'd had when he'd been human, sleeping in alleyways, squirreling away the money and goods he and the gang had stolen because Sam knew that the next few nights might not bring anything at all.

"So," he said. "Does any of this have to do with you hauling tail in this car before you picked me up?"

Corinna made another turn onto a remote road bursting with tulip trees and white fences. "Yup. Ned asked me to come to his place tonight, finally. But it was because his 'ex' would be out of town at a teaching conference and we'd have the house to ourselves. So we ate pizza until a surprise visitor strolled through the door. And, wouldn't you know it—this visitor got mad because there hadn't ever been a breakup." Corinna laughed. "She even called me a floozy. *Me.*"

The jealous pressure that had been building within Sam dispersed, leaving room for sympathy. "He's a dirtbag. Want me to talk to him?"

He was hungry anyway.

"No, Sam. Everything's done. He hustled me to the car as she yelled at him, and I burned rubber to leave him behind. I should've listened to my friends, huh?"

By this time, she had maneuvered the vehicle to the side of the cricket-serenaded road, where an oak shrouded them. She shut off the engine, possibly so she could use her hands to help tell the rest of her story.

"I mean, have you ever met a bigger loser?" she asked, spreading her thumb and forefinger then imposing the letter *L* on her forehead. "I've got to be the hugest chump ever."

"Well, you did make a strong statement by spitting gravel up with your tires and then flying out of his driveway like a bat out of heck," he said.

They laughed, and before Corinna even asked how he knew about the spitting gravel in the driveway, the cleansing sound faded.

He realized that they were in a car on a dark road. Together.

And he had almost forgotten that he'd thought about biting her tonight, just because it would make him feel better about Gisele's attentions to Edward.

Even though his wariness about the wisdom of that had returned, his appetite still expanded within his veins. But this was…nice. Listening to a June night, leaning his head against a car window.

Hanging out with the one person who'd ever given him a measure of peace.

"Sam?"

"Hmm?"

She had turned to face him, toying with the grass bracelet on her wrist.

"Do you realize I just kidnapped you?" she said jokingly.

His eyebrows shot up, and she laughed again.

"I told you," she said, "I've been doing goofy things lately. And don't worry—I'm not acting out some ex-boyfriend revenge fantasy just because you look like him."

"Then what are you doing?"

She bit her lip, obviously indecisive about something or another. But then, before Sam could process what was happening, she surged toward him, catching his lips with hers.

Immediately he went on high alert, his vision doused with scarlet, his body a storm of stirring blood. This was wrong: kissing a human. Because it would only end in a violent embrace that he would have to chase from her memory. *She* was even wrong for him: a possible sensitive who might know him for what he really was. Back when he'd been a post-civil war mortal, he probably would've even paused at their racial differences, but he hadn't learned at the time that humanity was under the skin, not on it.

But as the pressure of her lips eased into a softer touch, his blood raced with what he thought a sugar rush might feel like, if he could only remember. With each passing instant, he wanted more, and he would have done anything to get it.

His head pounded, mimicking his libido and his gums as his fangs began to ache and throb.

She pulled back slightly, their lips disconnecting in a leisurely sip.

"Your skin," she whispered. "It's always so cold—"

Out of self-preservation, he reached out to touch her temple, clouding her mind on a more than superficial level. Then afterwards, he said, "Sleep."

As his pulse flailed, her eyelids drooped and she fell back against the seat, lulled so he could escape.

But before he did, he stood by his open car door, risking one last look at her: hair spread like a dark angel's, her lashes fanned over her cheek, her chest rising and falling until her breasts tempted him to stay, to drink—

No.

"Wake up," he said before he sped away in a blur she would never see. Her car door creaked from the force of his departure.

He moved so fast that he darted into the air, flying for Lexington, where he would find someone else to ease his hunger. Another human's blood would be just as good, if not better.

And he kept trying to convince himself of that even as he landed in a remote parking area and segued into a fast walk toward the nearest street.

Toward the nearest bar that was sure to hold all kinds of choices for a vampire who hadn't gotten his fill tonight.

AT THE BEGINNING of the night, Edward had awakened to a wonderful sensation.

Warmth, just as if a serene simmer was burnishing him from the inside out. Truthfully, he hadn't felt this content in a long time, not since…

He allowed memories of his initial nights with the gang to hover for only a second before dismissing them. Back then, when he hadn't been the wiser, he'd interpreted the sensation as an answer to his emptiness.

But *this* warmth...

Where had it come from?

The fog from his rest lifted as he sat up and found himself in the middle of a heavy canvas tent, decorated in the same manner as the harem-attic. He was moored to the ground and buried in a mound of soft blankets that smelled of rose-petaled days gone by.

A soft breeze—fresh with summer grass and cool night—whispered against the tent, teasing the swaths of silk that draped from one corner to the other.

Gisele must have relocated him here, as if rewarding him for not fighting her as strongly as he should have last night, when she'd taken him outside to fly.

Or maybe she was thanking him for exposing that there was more to his quest for humanity than he had ever revealed before.

However, a good rest had cleared his mind enough so that he denied having those doubts about reclaiming his soul now.

Edward sank back into the blankets. If she was so intent upon rewarding him, he would continue her game, eventually hoodwinking her into taking these chains off one link at a time, if needed. Then...

Half-hidden by the thick material, Gisele rose from the other side of the large bed, sending his heartbeat pistoning. These chains—he couldn't tolerate how they robbed him of his warning senses.

"Ooo," she said, stretching like a pussycat.

Even in the darkness, he could see she was wearing

a short white nightgown that would've looked at home hanging on a clothesline during a sunny day. But Edward told himself that it was too innocent for her.

So why did she still look natural in it?

She plopped back down to the bed and leaned on her elbow, resting her head on a palm. "I assume you had a fine sleep?"

He had, but he wouldn't say it, mainly because he knew the reason he'd felt so warm and toasty now. Gisele, his creator, had been near.

A woman who should've been the bane of his existence.

She made it even worse when she guessed what he'd been thinking.

"This is the way it would be with us," she said, lavishing a long gaze upon him. "A touch of reassurance while we rest, the possibility of an embrace when dusk arrives. Just knowing that we have each other nearby. It is only right for us to wish to be near each other."

"Stephen and the boys eventually slept by themselves, away from Fegan."

"Not Sam. He honored his instincts." She pushed herself back upward, a serious cast to her expression. "Stephen, in particular, was a rebel, but you would know that as his good friend. Is he faring well now that he is human?"

"You two didn't get on very brilliantly, Gisele. Why would you care?"

She took his brusqueness in stride. "Stephen was my adopted brother. We quarreled, yes, but when it came down to it, I looked out for him and he did the same for me."

Edward lackadaisically stretched his naked body, maybe just to play the game and fool her into thinking he might come around to all this creator/created nuttery.

Perhaps he could even get another length of chain off tonight if he was a good lad.

"Stephen and Kimberly have a son now since his restored humanity allowed it. Nate is two. Last I heard, they were working on producing another."

"So Stephen got what he wished for. He does not miss—"

"Being a vampire? Not remotely."

Edward tucked his hands beneath his head, and when he felt Gisele skimming a hot gaze over him, his skin tingled. He expected anger to swamp him, but it didn't. Not this time.

So he *forced* himself to hate the profound lust that was becoming all too familiar.

"A baby," Gisele said, drawing her knees beneath her dress and cradling them. "Did you ever want one, Edward?"

He found himself cocking his head at her, his defenses lowered. He quickly corrected the error.

"I?" he asked. "No. My father's betrayal in claiming me made me swear off children. I never even so much as wanted to make my own created."

Gisele fixed her gaze on one of the draped silks. "As a human, I was too young to decide whether I wanted a baby or not."

He found himself turning toward her. "You were too busy drinking coffees at sidewalk tables, seeing those movies and sleeping around."

"I think I only became maternal when Sam asked me to recreate him."

Her comment struck a chord of longing within Edward. Companionship. Intimacy.

The words buried themselves in his chest, finally

sinking in and rousing a hunger so strong that he grimaced from the pangs.

Lightning-quick, Gisele followed, plunging into his head as if chasing him down, then batting his memories around in order to familiarize herself with them. Afterward, she rolled them close to her so they didn't anguish him any more.

He held his breath at the warmth, the security.

But, then, as if sorry she'd crossed a line, she withdrew, leaving only an echo that he wished he could hold on to.

She sat there for a moment, her hand over her chest, as if shaken by what she'd seen within him.

Then she stood. "Terrence has been watching over us all day. I need to tell him to return home."

"Where you'll give him a treat?"

Her gaze snagged his, and he held his breath.

After a strangled beat, she glanced away, opened the tent flap, then went outside, where she surely would see to Terrence.

Soon, she was back, sitting too close.

"Would you like a feeding, Edward?" she whispered.

And he had the feeling that she wouldn't be offering her neighbor this time.

The human's blood had served its purpose, but she had to have seen in Edward's head that he wanted something more, especially after flying and looking at those lights last night.

The warmth from her proximity brought him to a boil.

"Edward," she repeated softly.

She turned her arm fleshy side up and sliced it, blood beading, then blooming.

Red…fangs…

Her.

Saliva dripped from his mouth while he lunged against his chains as forcefully as he could. She caught his long hair and, avoiding his silver, led his mouth to her wound, where he sucked, cradling her arm to him, losing himself in her.

Losing all his intentions in this need….

Her hand tightened in his hair as he drew deeper, deeper, his mind's eye flaring with images of scarlet smoke that wound through itself in a sultry dance.

"Yes," she whispered, moving with the rhythm of each suck. "Yes…"

Her flavor saturated every corner of his palate: sweet, sour, salty, bitter, savory. The mental smoke weaved every aspect together until Edward became a part of the mélange, as well, wisping into her every cell.

She winced with each pull, each prod into places she'd always closed off to all the others.

Light…

Rising…

With every draw, he gained strength, recognizing her taste from that night, two years ago, when they had exchanged blood. He worked himself into her mind, reading her just as she was reading him.

There were no words, just impressions: pounding, thrashing, pulsating crimson that melted through his body and, undoubtedly, into hers, poking, persuading those painful emotions that they had left behind to come out again.

She shifted, and that urged him to go further.

Pulling against those chains, he drew his mouth up her arm, his fangs scratching her, leaving a trail of blood he wanted to lap up later. Greedy, so greedy—

She blocked him by yanking back on his hair.

Their gazes connected, both of them heaving in air, both of their eyes aroused to a flaming lightness in the dark.

With one hand she tore at her bodice, exposing those breasts he had lusted after. Small yet full. Ripe for his mouth.

Cruelly—yes, she was redefining the word—she arched forward and brushed her nipple against his lips, then pulled away before he could catch it in his mouth. Her intake of breath trumped the crazy stamp of their heartbeats.

Then, teasing him with her nipple again, she laughed and he growled, all animal, no reason.

Yet it wasn't over. She made a cut with her nail just below the curve of her breast, guiding him to it.

Comfortable…finally warm…

He drank again, his hands in the air because the chains wouldn't allow them any more distance. But that didn't matter, because his mouth, his throat, his stomach was filling with her.

Unable to contain himself, he satiated himself while Gisele urged him on in their minds.

Yours, mine, she thought. *Ours.*

Yet he could detect her strength waning, because he was draining her, needing her so much. His skin was poisoning her, too, and when she pushed off him, coming to a crouch on the other side of the blankets and wobbling in a search for balance, he reached for her.

For more than the blood.

Weakened beyond her limits, she crawled to the flap, disappearing into the night, and he licked the blood from his lips, wanting, needing.

Stronger than ever, he thought, knowing her blood had made him that way, although the chains still held.

But as the wind howled outside and the taste of her became only a memory once again, he realized that he was also lonelier than ever now that he'd partaken of a fruit that should've stayed forbidden.

If her plan for taming included addicting him, she had certainly done the job.

8

In Gisele's head-spinning, knee-gelled state, she crawled the short distance from the tent to the house, leaving the door open so air came through the screen door. She collapsed in the kitchen until Sam came home after what seemed like an hour later, even though it had probably only been minutes.

Vulnerable… She had never been so thoroughly opened to another.

When Sam saw her, he sprinted over in a blur, his hand immediately going to the slice on her arm and healing it. "What happened?"

"My fault. Gave him…too much of my blood… And touched him…too much. Silver…"

"Crap." Sam dragged her all the way over to him and opened his own wrist without chiding her, although she knew he wanted to.

"I sense him outside," he said, "so you didn't give him enough to break out of those chains."

"True." She also felt Edward's presence—a trill that would not stop fluttering in her core.

As she drank from Sam—an act that made Gisele think of being wrapped in blankets and sipping warm milk—she mind-spoke to her created.

I will see to him after I regain strength.

No, Sam answered. *I think you'd best stay here. I'll check on him. Something tells me having you in the same area is going to excite him even more, and that's the last thing we need.*

He was right. Gisele could sense Edward's body calling to hers, even if the carnal summons was a reluctant one, tightening between them with a torturous draw.

But then Sam's blood took her over, saturating her body, her consciousness. She saw what he had done tonight: parked with a girl in a car, her black hair curling around her face as she lavished a shy gaze on him. Sam had liked being with her, although he had been baffled about the reasons for it. He had never been attracted to one of them and had never intended to be, either.

Then the dark-haired girl leaned over to kiss Sam and—

Gisele felt as if she had stuck her finger in a light socket, her connection to Sam blaring into a white sheet of nothingness.

She pulled her mouth away from her partner's arm, stronger now. "What happened to you tonight? Are *you* okay?"

"Sure." He did not look at her, instead placing his fingers to his own wound and closing it. "Why wouldn't I be?"

Why wasn't he saying any more than that? She and Sam shared everything.

Gisele tried once more. "You pushed me out of your head. You have never done that before."

"I'm not shielding from you now." Healed, he nonetheless kept his fingers near his pulse point, staring at the pale-pink of the wound. "I just didn't want to remember tonight. That's all."

"Why?" But even as she asked, she knew, and it was

At her name, a spot warmed in a place just off-center in Edward's chest, and he imagined an electric line traveling from there through the ground to where he knew Gisele was listening on the floor of the kitchen.

She must have sensed him thinking about her—his body heat gave him away, no doubt—and she entered the tent moments later.

Cheeks pink from Sam's blood, she had changed clothing yet again, this time wearing long opera gloves with a sheath that was more a slip than a dress, although the flushed material was thick enough to provide a modicum of modesty.

In spite of that, the ball of warmth in Edward's chest expanded, spreading rays to his limbs.

They stared at each other, his thoughts so mangled he couldn't even translate them.

"How does he look?" Gisele asked Sam. She'd been holding the gloves that she had been using before, and now she tossed them to her companion.

"He's still moored, but he's been working at the anchors. If you don't give him any more blood, yours will wear off soon enough and it won't matter. *If* you don't give him more."

Edward and Gisele hadn't unlocked gazes, and for the first time since being chained, he suspected he might be on more equal terms with her, due to her blood racing around his veins.

Gisele looked to Sam, leaving Edward lacking in a vague way. It was obvious the pair was communicating silently. Edward even heard the slight buzz of her side of the conversation—a first—and his skin tingled as a consequence.

Then the vibration stopped.

"All right," Sam said out loud, raising his hands in resignation.

He came back over to Edward while yanking on the gloves. "Okay, you. Gisele has this goofy idea about how maybe you might like to walk around some, so if you give me one false move…"

"I understand." But at the same time, he was thinking, *Move around? Does this mean the moorings are coming out?*

Edward's mind began to whir, his deeply engrained schemes set back into motion, but when Sam gave him the death gaze, he hid his intentions. He had no doubts that the other vampire really would kill him if he attempted to slay Gisele.

But Edward wanted his own dream just as much as Sam wished to preserve his.

So what would happen if Edward continued cooperating? Would he be given just one more freedom that could lead to his escape and another chance to slay Gisele?

At the latter, something in him crashed, just as if he'd been flying and had suddenly lost the ability to soar.

Gisele. Gone?

His chest seemed to crack open, but he fought to shut it. He couldn't be that vulnerable, that…exposed to his enemy.

No, he would make her think that he was softening and, from there, he would fulfill his greatest dream.

As Sam yanked the moorings from the floor, Edward held up his hands in acquiescence, submissive.

But the emptiness within him spread, making him realize that, more than anything, he wanted to fly with her again.

And that made an escape more necessary than ever.

FORGIVENESS.

As Gisele had leaned against the kitchen's screen door and listened to Sam and Edward sparring in the tent, she had snagged on that one little word.

A word that meant everything.

It had goaded her into showing Edward that she trusted him enough to allow him to move around, because she did already forgive him for pressing his advantage when it came to drinking her blood. She had permitted him to do it, and she should have known better than to grant someone who considered her an enemy such access.

But her craving for him had overruled everything; she had wanted the intimacy, the feel of him taking her in. And she knew without reservation that he had wanted it, as well.

Now, with Sam here to help keep Edward in check, she could show her reluctant vampire that they could take what they had experienced together and make it grow beyond imagination, even though, at times, she wondered if it would truly work.

In the corner of the tent, she had stowed a pair of gray trousers. She offered them, and he accepted. It was an olive branch, really, meant to convey that good things would be in store if he decided to cooperate.

Soon, she and Sam were guiding Edward to a peaceful spot she had found the other night: a cove of rocks watched over by a stately willow. The location overlooked Terrence Gorley's property down the hill, and the moon gave a glow to the horses standing still amongst the expanse of grass.

Edward sat on a flat rock, leg drawn up so he could rest a forearm on his thigh. The night caressed his naked torso and played with the length of his hair. Gisele's chest squeezed, as if it were attempting to wring something out of itself.

"This, I gather," Edward said to no one in particular, "is yet another show of faith."

Sam leaned against the trunk of the tree behind Edward. "Just try running."

"I'm content for the time being, thank you."

Edward's dry tone made Gisele bite back a smile. His sharp attitude could entertain her, even when it was aimed in her direction.

"About earlier tonight…" she said.

"Oh, yes," Edward finished. "I must remember my place. You are meant to dominate me as my creator, not serve as my personal fountain."

Sam spoke up. "Maybe his head isn't as thick as we thought."

Edward ignored the jibe. "You should understand something in return—I don't take well to your using my natural appetite to teach me lessons you believe I need to learn."

"I take it back," Sam added. "Edward, you do need some education about how to function among other vampires. Big-time."

Gisele played peacemaker, addressing Edward's concern. "I am still learning how to be in charge, how to handle the responsibilities of nurturing."

"Said the mother tiger to her cub," Edward parried.

Even Sam was watching her now, as if wondering how she might handle such cheek from Edward. Or perhaps he was asking himself if she *would* ever learn how to handle her created family, but she did not go into his head to find out.

Edward picked up a small rock and tossed it down the hill. The sound of its landing echoed, rustling the grass.

"To be fair though," he said, "I tend to wonder what your own creator could possibly have taught you about nurturing."

All the devastation of her birth rushed back, but Edward added something that took her aback.

"It was wrong, what that beast did," he said. "I don't know his reasons, but there couldn't have been one good enough."

He said it with such conviction that she melted a bit, not out of passion or lust, but out of...

She did not know, but it left a sharp, hopeful pain behind.

Sam had even come to look at Edward with surprise, then he pushed off from the tree and wandered away as if to give them privacy while still remaining close.

Edward seemed to catch himself, straightening his spine as he cleared his throat. "He crossed a line that every vampire acknowledges, and that's not to be countenanced. Not from him...not from me."

Was he somehow...apologizing? She got the feeling it was about his rogue activities though—no more, no less.

She sat on the same flat rock he occupied. "You are not like my creator. *You* are able to admit you were wrong."

A dark smile captured his mouth. "I still wish to take my revenge on you, so I doubt you'll be saying that for long."

It was as if the cord they had formed earlier had been broken.

After tonight, after she had shared so much of herself, he still wanted to kill her.

But then her consciousness sought his again, just as

if it fed off being rejected and treated badly. Yet had that not always been the way with her?

He had turned to watch her, but it was not with the disgust she expected. There was regret somewhere in the depths of the amber gaze glowing in the night.

"Do you not *ever* feel differently, Edward?" she asked softly. "Do you not ever wish…?"

"That I would change my mind and join your happy little clan?"

He paused for so long that she read what she wanted to into the hesitation.

Which made his answer even more disappointing.

"No." Edward fixed his gaze on the countryside again, and his apparent wistfulness made her think that perhaps they would be able to work this out. But then he shook his head, as if fighting off the possibility. "I can comprehend the reason you turned me—believe me, I understand all too well—but I can't live with it."

"Because I am too much like you."

"Neither one of us is quite so deserving of forgiveness."

She did not accept this—not after what had transpired during their feeding. "Are you saying that we do not deserve any happiness? Are you truly that black and white in your beliefs?"

"There's no changing what I have chosen to do." His tone darkened. "And there's no changing what you did, either."

She wanted to ask if there was any redeeming it.

Yet her question was quelled when he started to rise threateningly.

Sam immediately zoomed over, grasping the back of Edward's neck and pushing him away from Gisele.

For a moment, Edward seemed stunned that he had

lost his well-trained cool and made the aggressive move. His eyes almost pleaded with her to understand that he was not certain of what he was doing anymore.

Then, as if realizing that he had given away too much, he stared straight ahead, a soldier back in his chains of confinement.

Had she seen anything in his gaze after all? Or had she been imagining it?

"I told you," Sam said, his voice warped, "if you threaten her—"

In one quicksilver motion, she was next to Sam, gently touching his shoulder. He looked at her, his eyes blazing a livid blue.

The color died a little as he sensed that she thought he was being too hard on Edward. He eased up on their captive's neck, but still lifted him off the rock, setting Edward's feet on the ground, then roughly guiding the taller, yet presently weaker, vampire toward the house.

"Hope this is still part of your plan, Gisele," Sam said.

She joined them, trying not to ignore how Edward kept his head down as they returned to their hideaway.

"Not to worry," she said, unwilling to give up. Not when she was so close to persuading him. She *had* to be. "I know what I am doing."

As always, Sam glanced at her as if he knew better.

9

SAM ENDED UP chaining Edward to the floor of the almost-bare family room near the lone piece of furniture—a skeletal couch that lacked cushions—-hence depriving Edward of a bed and all the silken comfort of the attic or tent.

Then Gisele and Sam quickly covered every window so as to keep sunlight from scorching Edward at the onset of dawn.

For the next few nights, Sam brought bowls of still-warm blood for meals—blood that carried the taste of their neighbor.

Otherwise, they left Edward alone.

Smart move, that. Isolation forced him to crave Gisele, to obsess about how perfect she had felt under his mouth and hands, how her flavor had awakened something dangerously vulnerable within him.

He also had a lot of time to think about why Gisele would try to ease his guilt about going rogue.

She had seemed to understand just why he had gone to such lengths, and Edward couldn't grasp that. *No* one should be able to empathize, especially the vampire he had to kill.

Edward heard footsteps, then saw Sam. He was wearing the gloves and coming to retrieve the porcelain bowl that Edward had already drunk clean after awakening.

"I hope you don't mind me saying that I far preferred the initial accommodations that were offered," Edward said.

The other vampire looked ever so disappointed in his reluctant comrade. Sam also had a growing, disgruntled energy about him, and Edward suspected it had something to do with that human girl at the bridge.

"You're the one who blew your five-star stay," Sam said. "But that's what happens when you're as myopic as a horse's arsehole."

Hearing the other creature say it had a sobering effect. Sam had been the whip-smart youngster who had brought the gang into the modern age, and for the few decades Edward had been around him, he had always kept a sly ear open for Sam's input.

But revenge was all Edward had right now—it drove him, gave him a purpose.

A terrible thought insinuated itself in his chest. If he let his hatred go, what would become of him? What would he be?

"I've always stood for ideals," Edward said, reassuming his comfortable anger. "Can you say as much, Sam?"

The younger vampire frowned, showing Edward that his words had carried their desired effect.

But he pressed on, battling to keep that hatred burning bright within him. "Haven't you got anything you would stand for, as well? A goal that you want so badly it takes over your every thought and action?"

"No."

"There's nothing? *No one?*" Edward carefully slid the last part in. Divide and conquer. If he could play upon Sam's obvious distractions and somehow get him out of the house to that bridge, Gisele would be that much weaker.

"Not even your favorite girl? She seems to have distracted you quite handily."

"Shut up. I mean it." Sam's voice was level, just like a smooth stretch of road just before a collapse.

"We all need something to keep us going, mate. Because without it, we might as well be revenants who climb out of a coffin each night, brainlessly search for food, then hop right back in until the next dusk comes 'round."

"One more word, Edward, and those silver chains go in your mouth with a gag to keep them there."

Touchy cuss. Yet Sam's temper would only help Edward.

"A chain appetizer would be inhospitable, indeed," he said. "Don't mind if I refuse it."

He closed his eyes, feigning the need for rest. Divide and conquer.

He felt Sam leave the room, so Edward subtly pulled against the chains' moorings, detecting a slight give. Even though the blood he'd drunk from Gisele the other night had been diluted with the recent sustenance from that bowl, he could still feel her within him, as if she had settled low in his gut and in his limbs.

He was stronger, but not strong enough yet.

Giving himself over to restful fancy, he pictured what it might be like to break free so he could pounce on Gisele—

Edward's eyes opened, his heartbeat quickening as heat hissed through him. He should be imagining how sweet it would be to stake her, then tear out her heart, yet here he was reacting like an angry lover merely to the thought of her name.

He had to get out of these chains before he lost his purpose—his true self—altogether.

From the kitchen, the clatter of a bowl being heaved against a counter broke the night air.

Sam.

Poor, frustrated Sam, who had probably been peeking out the window and looking in the direction of that bridge.

Edward tugged at the chains and worked them against the moorings, feeling the anchors give just that much more.

IN THE ATTIC, where she lay on the blanket bed with her cheek pressed to silk, Gisele heard the bowl smash apart in the kitchen.

Based on the goading she had overheard from Edward downstairs, she understood Sam's ill mood, and she wished she could somehow help him. But he had become caught up in a human, something she had always avoided.

If only she were as clear on what to do with Edward.

From the start, her choices had been twisted when it came to him, and she had no idea why. Common sense dictated that she terminate him, since she could not set him free just to attack her again, yet the thought of ending his existence was as inconceivable as amputating a portion of her own self.

She ran her hand over the indentation in the material next to her, caused by the weight of Edward's body, then she fisted the silk, making the phantom presence disappear.

I still wish to take my revenge on you, he'd told her.

She had thought he was coming around, but he had corrected that notion in no uncertain terms. That, and

Sam's growing distance, was why she had stayed away the past few nights, rethinking this taming.

Footfalls sounded on the attic steps. They were Sam's.

Pushing away from the silks, she stood, awaiting him as he came through the open door.

He looked haggard for a vampire, but maybe it was just his eyes.

"You know what we should do soon?" she asked, wishing to cheer him. "Hit a bar. Together. Just to perk up our nights."

Sam actually smiled, but it soon waned. "That won't be happening any time soon. I thought I might just dart out to the woods tonight, take a creature for dinner, then get right back here."

"Oh, dear. You know what that means."

He raised an eyebrow at her teasing tone.

"It signifies," she said, "that we have become geriatric before our time. It's the vampire version of eating food that does not upset our systems at four in the afternoon, then going to bed by eight. We need some spice again."

"So go out and get yourself some tonight," he said. "I don't mind staying here to watch Edward."

And how about the next night? she wanted to ask. *And the next?*

She reached out to touch Sam's spiky hair, but she hesitated, not knowing quite why.

They both noticed, so she went ahead and ruffled his short sandy strands. For some reason, it broke what she had of a heart when he glanced away.

She crossed her arms over her chest, covering the spot under her breast where she had sliced a cut for Edward to drink several nights ago. It was healed now, but still felt open as far as she was concerned.

"This cannot have happened with us," she said. "This awkwardness."

Sam shrugged, but she knew his casual gesture was a cover for so much more.

"The thing is," he said, "even if you did away with Edward, he'd still be here…there…wherever we ended up afterward."

"Yes, he would." Because they could never escape the questions he had brought up lately—about who they were now, about how much they needed each other in their own ways.

And obviously Sam felt as if he had come out the loser, didn't he?

"What can I do to improve matters?" she asked. "How can I make things as they used to be with us?"

Sam paused, started to answer, then stopped. He shrugged again as his gaze strayed toward the covered attic window.

She did not have to peer into his mind to know that he was thinking of the girl.

Gisele took his hand, as if trying to keep him here with her. "I heard Edward talking to you downstairs. He is encouraging you to go to the bridge again, but only because he is hoping to force us apart."

"I know. And it was kind of working."

There was a break of anguish in Sam's voice, and Gisele connected to it because she felt the same way about Edward.

Both she and Sam wanted something that might destroy them in the end.

"What is it about her?" Gisele asked. "Why this girl?"

"Corinna?"

Corinna. A glimpse into his mind told her everything she needed to know: dark, gorgeously lush hair. Nearly black eyes that seemed liquid in their gentleness. Smooth skin with a dusting of youthful freckles.

But…strange. Knowing the depth of his need for the girl made Gisele wish he *would* go to that bridge, because she could also feel his joy at the possibility.

"Corinna makes you laugh and smile," Gisele said softly. "She makes you think you will never be hungry or at a loss again."

"Yeah," Sam said. "That's about the gist of it."

Gisele swallowed hard. Hadn't she felt a startling warmth when she had awakened next to Edward? Didn't she see a reflection of herself in him?

He kept her company in their shared darkness. He was the other half she'd been lacking.

She fisted her hands in Sam's, wishing she were wrong, but knowing beyond a doubt that she had hit on the truth.

"But," Sam said, still dwelling on the girl from the bridge, "I know the best option is to move on from Corinna and deal with Edward. He's a point of survival. She isn't."

Gisele did not question his resolution, because they needed to find normalcy again.

Needed it badly.

"Seriously," Sam added, "I've got it all covered here if you want to shake things up and grab a bite in town. I know you like the hustle and bustle. Besides, there're bridges I'd rather avoid by going too far out the door, if it's all the same to you."

"If you are certain," she said, trying to whip up some excitement for the hunt. "Then, thank you, Sam."

"For what?"

"For…" She smiled. "For you."

Their hands disconnected as Sam grinned, then went back downstairs.

After a moment of getting used to his absence, she descended to the bedroom and began primping for town. However, she was not as excited about this as she should have been. Hunting alone held no attraction for her. She worked best with a partner.

An image consumed Gisele: her feeding Edward again, his lips sucking her to a heady weakness....

She tossed down her brush, which she had been using to smooth her hair back from her face. Running her hands down the black miniskirt and tight mock turtle-neck top she had plucked from a bedroom drawer, she slid a pair of slingback, peep-toe, leopard heels on, then made her way to the family room.

Sam was sitting against a paneled wall facing Edward, who was slumped back against the foot of the bare-bones couch, looking much weaker than she suspected him of being.

Her skin tightened with bumps as she felt him watching her, devouring. Ravishing.

The hair on her arms rose to attention, her sex going tight.

Sam jerked his chin at her wardrobe. "Whoever lived here sure had some collection. All shapes, all sizes, and all that eastern-type stuff in the trunks. Then there's these hot-mama clothes."

"I think an actress spent some time in this house—professional or maybe only delusional." She had to concentrate on getting her words out, because Edward's silent, intense attention was making her skim over the frames of her consciousness, like a movie sent into fast forward.

"Well, have a good time," Sam said.

"Be kind to those poor meals out there," Edward added, and she knew it was because he was dead set on forcing her gaze on him.

She tried not to acknowledge him, but resisting was fruitless.

As she glanced at him on her way to the door, she caught something unexpected, and her blood lurched in her limbs, almost taking her out at the legs.

Emotion in his eyes. Desire. Lust.

And something more that she could not even begin to describe….

He grimaced then turned away, setting reality back on course. Yet what she had seen in his gaze lingered.

What had it been?

"Back soon," she said to Sam.

"Take your time, but just know that the longer you're gone, the more tempted I'll be to drive that stake into his black heart."

Sam offered a kidding smile, although she would not rule out a possible staking with the way Edward had been antagonizing him about Corinna before. But, luckily, her partner was strong, and she had faith in his willpower.

"An hour," she said.

Then, with a wink at Sam, she bolted out the door and flew to Lexington, to a collegiate bar near campus where the males would be randy and easy to lure.

Finally, she could focus on something other than Edward.

Brushing the name out of her head, she talked to a bouncer who invited her inside. After showing a fake ID that she adjusted every five years, she got into the mood, telling herself she was hungry for blood and for a pick-me-up in spirits.

She scanned the brass-studded, dark-wood-paneled room with its dartboards and a moose head over the bar itself. Rock music from a jukebox blended with heartbeats, and too much cologne and beer wafted in the air, diffusing her sense of smell, but not enough to matter.

All the while, she kept chasing off what she had seen in Edward back at the house.

What *was* it?

Across the darkened floor, a gaggle of young, well-heeled men who were no doubt attending summer university classes did their best to seduce local girls. Among them, she spotted justified prey, and zeroed in on his hundred-dollar haircut, his designer button-down and loafers, his expensive wristwatch.

And the heavy ring he wore that still carried a trace of blood, perhaps from a punch to someone else's face.

He had a petite blond girl against a wall in a corner, and her eyes were darting around, seeking an escape. When he bent down to whisper into her ear, she finally ducked away from him, heading across the floor toward the bar's door.

When he shoved a rude gesture at her retreating back, Gisele advanced, slipping into the same corner the girl had deserted.

When he turned back around to find Gisele there, he startled.

"Hi," she said, her voice in sway mode.

"Hi there," he said, leaning his beer-fisted arm against the wall and over her, trapping her even more thoroughly than the previous female.

He was not drunk, this boy. As she quickly skimmed

him just enough to read his intentions, she saw that alcohol was a prop as well as an enticement used to put his own victims at a disadvantage.

Gisele anticipated the flood of stimulation she should have felt by now, but it never came. Instead, she kept seeing Edward's gaze blocking out the boy in front of her.

She blinked, trying to get back to form.

Blood, she thought. *Back to the blood and the arousal and the hunt.*

"This music is loud," she said, putting her hand on his arm. "Would you like to go outside?"

He looked as if he had hit gold. "Sure."

Again, she awaited the rush.

None.

It was not long before she had him out of the bar, against a wall in a shadowed brick alley. But when she pressed her body against his, her stomach turned.

Edward's eyes…

Being away from him, drinking from another, was not right at all, not any more. She had no enthusiasm for this, no taste….

She backed away, but the prey grabbed both her arms, whirring her around and plastering her against the wall.

"You a tease?" he asked, driving his crotch against her and dropping his plastic cup of beer to the ground so it splashed against her legs. "I sure hope not."

He gave her a mild yet stinging slap, which she took in numb acceptance. She should not have come tonight, should not have left Edward.

But in the here and now, the prey's eyes loomed in her gaze, and they provided such a contrast to Edward's that it was a shock to her system.

This was the look of someone who would hurt her, and it made her wonder if Edward really did have it in him to carry through with his threats after what had come between them the past week—

The prey's rough hand was headed under her skirt, but Gisele had tolerated enough. She wanted to go back.

She knocked his hands away from her and swiftly picked him up by his shirt collar, holding him up until his feet were kicking in the air. As he choked, he gripped her wrists.

"Little boy," she said, "after tonight, you are going to find yourself hesitating ever to act that way with a woman again. You will not recall just why that is, but you *will* change your habits."

With that, she guided him around to the wall with much more care than he deserved, then pinned him there.

"One less of you on the street," she whispered, touching the boy's temple in order to soothe him back to normal.

When she was done, she propped the boy just inside the bar's backroom door, making certain no one saw her. Then, as if making up for lost time, she flew back to the hideaway.

Bent on seeing just what *had* been in Edward's eyes.

EDWARD and Sam hadn't uttered a word to each other since Gisele had left, mostly because Edward had the feeling his ex-comrade would stake him if he said anything more about the girl by the bridge.

And he was too close to getting free to risk that.

He felt the chains' moorings give yet another fraction on his right side, but Sam, who sat across the room staring at a velvet-curtained window, was too distracted to notice. He had even taken off his gloves to slap them against his leg, as if that could force the slow passage of time.

Edward took an instant to rest from his efforts. Just another hour and he might have it….

Think of Gisele coming home from the hunt, he told himself. *She comes through the door, and she doesn't see you waiting in the shadows for her and...*

His cock went stiff, and he paused at the unwanted reaction. To make things even worse, a dark spot flared in the middle of his chest as he thought about her out there hunting. It had been bothering him since she'd left, wearing that provocative dress and those want-me-baby shoes.

The very idea of her touching someone else, laying her mouth against another neck…It tore him down the middle, and he knew she had seen his envy before she had gone.

Maybe that was why he was trying so diligently to escape now.

He doubled his quiet efforts to free himself, but when the back door crashed open and Gisele sped into the room, he stopped, his blood all but coming to a halt, as well.

Why was her presence enough to take him over?

He didn't have time to consider an answer as her hair drifted from the air back down to her shoulders, as the room settled to order from her abrupt entrance.

Sam stood, his miles-away stare interrupted.

"Sam," she said, her voice controlled, even over the tiny quake Edward detected beneath the surface. "Would it be too much to ask for me to be alone with Edward for a time?"

Sam's shoulders went stiff as he moved toward the door.

Gisele took a step toward Sam. Then, clearly keeping herself from closing the remaining distance, she brought her hand to her chest.

Sam glanced back before opening the door, and Edward suspected that they were linked mind-to-mind.

He had no idea what was said, but he could tell from the way Sam hunched that he felt rejected.

It should've been a glorious sign for Edward. Divide and conquer.

But when Sam closed the door behind him, Gisele looked just as devastated. Lost.

A beat passed, and in spite of himself, Edward connected with her sorrow.

Will he ever come back...? she was thinking.

Gisele sensed Edward in her mind, but instead of reprimanding him for the invasion, she seemed to search his gaze instead.

Burned, Edward glanced away and blocked his thoughts, afraid of what she might find.

Finally, she spoke. "Sam does not like to be left in the cold," she said.

"I'm sure he would kill me before that happened."

She carried on with whatever agenda had brought her back from the hunt so soon. "I will not choose between you or him, Edward. Not when I would need to have eyes in the back of my head for the rest of my nights if I were to unchain you."

He didn't confirm or deny that, even though something deep inside him told him to look at her again, to show her she might not have to make such a choice, after all. Not after what he had learned about himself—and maybe even her—these past nights.

He killed that voice, knowing it was wrong. How

could he live with himself if he gave up all his lofty ideas of justice?

If he gave up his soul?

He dragged his gaze back to her, and he knew she could understand what was there, probably even better than he could. She seemed to drink in as much as possible, then took a step closer, as if encouraged.

"Would I have to worry if I unchained you?" she asked.

"Yes," he said, unwilling, unprepared…unable to say no.

She looked as if she didn't believe him. "If I were to free you, you would indeed kill me? Or are you terrified that you would not be able to carry through with it?"

"I would—" he started.

"Because that would turn your world upside down, wouldn't it, Edward?"

Red began to veil his gaze, but it wasn't because he was caught up in desire.

It was from blinding fear that she was right.

Still, he fought back, because that was all he knew. "You would never release me, because *you're* afraid I would run away without ever looking back."

"I suppose there is only one way to see."

Her answer stunned him, and when she walked to where Sam had been sitting and picked up the gloves he had stripped off earlier, he thought he might have misheard her.

Yet she put on those gloves and walked toward him, even as he desperately worked at his moorings.

And they were giving way, offering hope that he would win this fight, win back…

His soul?

What did a soul mean now?

But he never had the chance to free himself, because with one super-speeded motion, Gisele tore the moorings from the floor and the chains from around his neck and wrists, leaving him free.

Then she backed up, taking off the gloves and throwing them to the ground like gauntlets.

Edward sucked in a few cleansing breaths, unfettered, liberated.

The choice was his.

Gisele, who filled him sexually...and even more than only that?

Or a soul?

Instinctively, Edward's blood boiled, his vision shrouded by a red so deep that all he saw were old patterns that had always driven him.

The old desires that had kept him going even as he wished every bit of them would die.

His true monster came out, fanged and livid, and he sprang into the air, launching himself at her, regret chasing right after him.

10

EDWARD CLOSED in on Gisele, his fangs ready, his fingers clawed.

But even with the sinking feeling that pressed her down, she was prepared.

From the depths of her anguish, she summoned her own monster, just as horrendous as his, then flew into the air to block him.

They met with a bone-jarring crash, him bringing down his claws to rip at her, her bringing up her hands to brace against his arms.

They strained against each other, pulses hammering, eyes flaring, muscles burning with last-stand power as they hovered in the air. It was enough time for Gisele to realize that his released rage was making up for the silver poison that remained within him.

Why does it have to be this way? Why, Edward?

He was too far gone to open up to her, but she could have forced the issue and entered his head. Her abilities were still greater, yet she had hoped she would not have to use them.

That he would stay even without the chains.

Their muscles began to quiver with the effort of holding each other back, so Gisele let go just long enough to use his momentum to flip him toward the wall, where she pinned him with her hands and knees, his bare back to the paneling.

Inches away from Edward's face, the sharp end of a decorative rod holding up a set of dark velvet curtains gleamed, and he glanced at it, then at her.

He smiled, all fang.

"Edward," she said, unable to hold back her sorrow.

A flash of remorse shone through his glare, but then he erased every remnant of it by hissing, "What did you think I would do?"

Her vision went black, just like a movie that blurred to its conclusion on the screen.

But then she recovered, survival taking over as she levered him toward the pointed end of the curtain rod, which was now a slice away from his face.

What else can I do? she thought, desperate for an option.

Any other option.

She spoke aloud. "Do not make me kill you. Please."

"Why are you so reluctant?" he ground out.

It was almost as if he were asking her to get this over with. She did not know for certain, though, because his mind was still closed.

But it would not always be that way, right? She had seen it in his eyes.

"You do not want me to go through with this," she said, her throat going tight.

He turned his gaze on the curtain rod. "Just do it, Gisele. Put us both out of our misery."

No.

She eased up on him, then slid them both down the wall a meter, creating distance between them and the sharp rod. She pressed her face to his chest, his skin a balm to her.

Or perhaps truly a poison…

Words barely made it out of her throat. "We can find a way to stop this."

His breathing suspended, and her pulse beat stronger with hope.

But then he stiffened, and she knew he was not going to surrender.

He struck out, heaving her away from him and making her whirl away through the air. At the same time, he dove to the floor, where he rolled to a crouch, his fingers clawed and ready for her again.

Halting her spin, she dropped to the floor, too, refusing to engage unless he came at her.

"I see," she said, her voice trembling, even though she wrestled to smooth it out. "You will fight until the bitter end, even if there could be a solution."

"A…solution?" His laugh was serrated—and so very hollow—as he crept along the floor, circling, forcing her to turn just to keep facing him. "What's the scenario you picture? How about this: We settle down, say, in a posh spot like Knightsbridge. We take tea with a dollop of blood in it for flavoring every dusk and attend a West End show once a week. Afterward, we shed the civility and hunt together, wreak some carnage and call it a night before you chain me back up to the wall. Yes, sounds lovely."

She tried not to cringe.

"Can't you see we need each other?" she whispered, because it had to matter. More than any of this. "Can't you see that no one else will ever do for either of us?"

He came to a standstill in mid stalk.

"Need," he said, tilting his head, the bewildered gesture at odds with the monstrous face he wore, the fangs and feral eyes and claws.

"Yes," she said, barely daring to breathe. "Tonight, during my hunting, I could barely stand to be away from you. I cannot imagine what it would be like if you left for good—or if you perished. Can you tell me you do not feel the same way?"

Edward was already shaking his head, as if to dislodge what she had planted there.

"Be with me," she said, standing now, her monstrous face receding, fangs slipping back into her gums. "If you stay, I promise—*I* would never turn my back on you. No betrayals, Edward. I would perish before ever hurting you again."

As he stared at her, she rested her arms at her sides, open to any attack that might come—any punishment for hurting him in the first place.

"I am sorry for everything I have done to you," she said. "More sorry than you can know."

He bared his fangs, backing away from her. "Sorry isn't enough. It'll never be enough."

But she had meant it, and she wished he could see just how deeply.

"I am sorry to hear that, too," she said.

He started to stand, his eyes gentling, and hope—a near stranger—suffused her.

But then he fisted his hands, as if remembering. Always remembering….

Before she knew it, he had darted up to the curtain rod, stripping it from its brackets in a screech of metal. Bracing his feet against the wall, he furiously launched himself back at her.

But Gisele was not going to fight any more, and she merely faced the assault, waiting…clinging to her last bit of faith in what she had seen in his eyes earlier.

He will not kill me, she thought, as if it were a spell that might save her. *I know he will not—*

Edward landed meters away with a thud, the floor shaking as he cocked the curtain rod back in preparation to run her through. The velvet draped over his bare shoulder and, for a crazy moment, she saw him as the duke's bastard son who had bitterly turned away from humanity. Saw him as the confused vampire who had no idea where he could find light in the darkness.

Saw the pain that colored his every night.

In a final act of taming, Gisele opened her arms, still believing he would not carry through.

We have so much together, she cried out with her mind. *Do you hear me, Edward…?*

He drove the rod forward, and she saw it coming as if in slow motion. Then, as it got closer, his gaze widened, and, in its depths, she witnessed the best moments of their last few nights together: flying through the sky and coming upon those city lights, crimson smoke fusing them as they touched each other so intimately—

With a sharp cry, he stopped the rod from impaling her, and Gisele nearly imploded with joy.

But Edward released a yell of frustration and swung the curtain rod at her instead.

She dodged it effortlessly, but he targeted her again, the velvet rippling and slithering around both of them as she continued to avoid the improvised club.

Finally, with one swift move, she clutched at the curtain and yanked, tearing the pole from his grasp forcefully enough that one of the pointed ends speared into the floor. The jerk of the curtain tangled around their bodies and brought them both off balance, giving Edward a last chance to spring at her.

As he knocked her to the floor, he circled his hands around her throat, and she allowed it, gasping for breath.

He will not go any further, she told herself. *I lay my existence on it....*

But even though she did not retaliate physically, she instinctively defended herself mentally, opening her mind so wide that he pitched forward and lost his grip on her neck, as if something had given way beneath him.

She caught him and rolled over, hunching over him, the velvet cocooning their bodies as his mind accidentally melded with hers in ultimate warmth, security....

He did not struggle to get out. Perhaps he was too weak from his exertions.

On full mental power, she immediately sought out his painful memory of the cave where she had exchanged with him on that first pivotal night. The Marie Antoinette painting that the gang had filched from a collector's home loomed over the carousel horses, the gold and gems, the booty they had collected over the years.

Then she guided Edward over to a throne, where a hill of dust was piled on the seat cushion.

"Fegan," she heard Edward whisper.

She had taken him back to the moment when he had just killed his maker—the terrible instant when she had roared out from the shadows, hurt and shocked, to take her revenge on the vampire who had murdered her surrogate father.

"If I could take this moment back," she whispered to him, "I would do so. I should have let you go."

The vision tilted, showing Edward falling to his knees,

convulsing, and she knew this was the moment he had become human again—before she had robbed him.

In a bid to revise their history, the dream-Gisele stayed away from him, even though it tore her apart. If she had left him this way, she would never have tasted him, never have felt what she had come to feel….

Her belly contracted so violently from the hunger for him that it yanked her out of the vision, bending her double. It destroyed their mind-link, tossing them back to the here and now, where they were still in fighting position, her on top of him, both of them swathed in the heavy curtain.

She had given him up in the vision, but now, with him here, so close, so available…?

She dug her fingernails into her palms, drawing blood, stopping herself.

She wouldn't bite him now. Not after trying to get him to trust her.

Below her, his vampire features mellowed back into his more human-like ones, and his lips parted, his eyes a dark cloud that she could not read.

Gisele prepared to crawl off of him. *Need to leave before it is too late….*

"I only wish," she said, pushing away from him, "that I could turn back time and make that vision real."

Edward grasped her wrists, as if unwilling to accept even her sincerest apologies.

And she could not blame him.

HE HADN'T been able to do it.

Success had been within such easy reach, the curtain rod a gasp away from striking through her heart, but he had failed.

Edward couldn't comprehend it, and when Gisele had welcomed the attack without fighting back, it had made him even more baffled.

He wasn't even certain of the reason he was holding on to her, not letting go.

Had he come to want her more than his old desires? No, it couldn't be true.

"You intend to leave this fight," he said.

She seemed so resigned, a Gisele he wasn't familiar with. "If I walked out the door, I hardly think you would follow—not even to kill me, Edward."

He realized that his fingers were banding her where the silver had bound him, and he released her.

He was free to leave even if he didn't have the guts to carry through with killing her. This could be their compromise—his return to grace.

But he pulled her back on top of him, making her sit on his belly, their chests moving in rhythm, attuned to each others' patterns by now.

He became all too aware of the flesh of her thighs skimming the sides of him, and...

Ah, her sex. She wasn't wearing knickers, and he could feel the humid folds of her opening against his bare belly.

She hadn't done it by design or seduction, either, and that made it all the more enticing.

The last vestiges of his anger dissipated as lust—that's all it was, that's all it could be—enflamed him.

He bared his teeth, wrapping the fingers of one hand around her neck again. She took it in stride.

"Squeeze," she said. "Show me you are serious about doing it, or do not do it at all. Either way, this ends now."

He tightened his fingers, but there didn't seem to be a good enough justification for this anymore.

Nothing was the same, nothing made sense.

Let go, something deeply buried told him. *You want to, but you hate knowing it.*

Meanwhile, Gisele had come to double over again, the ache of her hunger strong. She pushed his hand away, starting to rise off him, when he made a grab for her.

Then, fire in her eyes, she took hold of him, quickly planting his hand over his head and angling his other one up to join it.

The motion slid her up his belly and to his stomach, and he groaned at the feel of her sex riding over him. His body primed itself, always her victim, even a willing one.

She was responding, too—fangs, eyes, everything aroused.

And that was all it took.

Mind in a fury, he used all his strength to surge up to a sitting position and latch his mouth to one of her breasts, where the velvet had draped away from the luscious curve covered by her tight top. Perhaps he'd meant to tear at the material and the flesh beneath, but he didn't.

No, he didn't.

Taken aback, Gisele still held on to his hands, even as he gnawed at her through the thin cloth. Her nipple had already gone hard, and he could hear her wince as his fangs scraped and his tongue bathed her through the cotton.

"What do you want from me?" she asked.

Everything, he thought. *And only you have ever been able to provide that.*

He sucked her harder, and she heaved in a breath. His growing erection strained against his trousers, dizziness compounding the remaining silver weakness in his bloodstream.

Gradually, he was able to work one of his hands free

from her grip and trail it up the inside of her arm, then down over the side of the breast he was laving and over her ribs until he placed it at her back to press her chest closer to his mouth.

He wanted her inside of him, always. Wanted every inch, every pulse, every shared memory that made him feel more alive than he had felt as a human.

Clearly, she was still on alert, keeping a grasp on his other hand while gauging what his intentions were. But he could tell she was melting, just as *he* was melting into *her.*

Bliss, he thought, finally not wishing he were somewhere else or that he could be *someone* else.

He traveled his hand lower, over the swerve of her ass, then below her skirt.

She gasped, grappling at the curtain that draped over them with her free hand and liberating them both a little more.

He came up for a breath and slicked a finger into her folds from behind, finding her clit and massaging. It had been a very long time since he had touched a female in this way, and he was rediscovering the mystery, the pleasure.

So soft, so wet…

She sounded like a kitten as she moved with his explorations, and after she shoved the curtains off even more, he pushed her backward, onto the pile they'd made.

The movement had lifted her skirt above her hips, and while they still gripped hands on the one side, he removed his fingers from her and brought his other hand to her front, working her to drenched abandon from there, instead.

The sight of the patch of dark hair between her legs, the pink center of her, kicked up Edward's desire. He had fed off the blood in that bowl earlier, but it had done nothing for him.

Gisele was the only one who could stop the rumblings by bringing out the emotions he'd buried.

He coaxed a finger inside her, and she rocked against him. Then, the unexpected happened.

Eyes unfocused, she used her free hand to pull him down for a fang-nipped kiss.

Edward's sight seemed to splatter at the touch of her lips, the heady taste of her, the desperate sips and draws.

He groaned and stroked another finger into her.

She answered by groaning back and deepening their kiss, avoiding fangs and sliding her tongue into his mouth to flirt with his own, to mimic the cadence of his fingers inside her.

In, out…around…

Hot and wet, like building steam pushing at him.

Mindlessly, he slid his fingers out of her and took her leg, raising it to his shoulder. A curtain was hooked in the heel of her shoe, and the velvet licked against his back.

And when he bent down to her sex, her heel dug into his skin, the soft-painful sensation driving him as never before.

She was threading her fingers through his hair, but she still held tightly to his other hand. It told him she didn't completely trust in what he was doing.

She had no reason to be on guard anymore, not when he merely wanted to please her, to smooth over her own bad memories with mental caresses.

He licked up the slit of her sex and shivered at her mind-exploding flavor, then went back for more, lavishing every spot with slow care, his consciousness pulsing.

When she cried out, he wondered if she was excited by the thought of his fangs in such a vulnerable place.

But it hadn't even occurred to him to strike, although it would be so easy.

He kissed her, loved her, delved into her with his tongue as her hips churned. He could feel her orgasm building within him, too, level by pounding level, turning his belly upside down in delightful anguish.

Pressure…pushing…pulling…

His gums throbbed, pained, pleasured, asking for more than any human sexual experience could ever provide.

More than any other woman could, as well.

It was as if something within Gisele was tugging at him now, drawing every single bit of his essence out. The tight agony was too much to control as they climbed together.

Up…faster. Up faster. Upfaster—

They rocketed upward, bodies bursting, then skidding, falling apart.

Then reforming with dizzying speed.

Breath… So hard to get. Blood… So impossible to control.

As he recovered, he realized that she had let go of his imprisoned hand, that the curtains had completely fallen away from them.

Free, he thought, catching his breath. Free to go.

But…

He didn't want to.

Instead, he sought her lips again, and as their passion flamed anew, their fangs clashed against each other, their kiss growing wild, frenzied, bloodied with wild cuts that would heal even before the taste of each other subsided.

She wrapped her legs around him, nestling against his cock, which was still hardened in his trousers.

He thrust against her, once, twice—

He could sense her losing it—every mental barrier was down, every defense. She fisted his hair, and he felt the same clutching hunger he'd always sensed in her.

But he wasn't going anywhere, he thought. Not now….

"Let it go," he said into her ear, a harsh whisper. "Just let it go."

"I…want…to…" she said.

He drove against her again, reaching down to undo his fly.

"Edward—" She sounded panicked as she pushed away from him. "My compulsions…I want your blood…want you in me that way, too…but I vowed I would not do it to you again…."

As she arched her neck back, her gaze was scrambled, on the edge of sanity.

In a flash, their minds melded, and he saw a replay of her biting him in that cave, of his dreams collapsing.

She didn't want to do it, he knew that, but when her gaze flared, he knew it was too late.

Her vampire nature—the chaos of their hunger—had taken her over. But in order to win him, she had promised to overcome her instincts, promised not to repeat that night when she had taken everything from him.

She had wanted to show him that they were better than mere beasts, but she couldn't, and that made Edward's hopes tumble until he felt lower than he'd ever thought possible.

If she couldn't help him see the glory of what he could be, then who could…?

With her higher strength, he couldn't resist her when she drove her fangs into him, then began sucking.

Mine, she was thinking with him, in him, completely over the edge. *Never going to let you leave.*

But even as his cock grew harder, images of that first bite consumed him.

His humanity…everything he'd worked so hard to attain…gone…

He pushed her away, breaking them apart as he reeled. Across from him, Gisele was covering her mouth with a trembling hand, her eyes full of horror.

"Edward," she said through her fingers. "I did not want—"

But he didn't wait around to hear anymore, instead stumbling out of the room and through the door into the night, fleeing from her, getting away from a situation that could never work, not in a thousand years.

At the same time, in the back of his head, he heard Gisele start to weep at seeing yet another one leave— the one that really mattered.

I am sorry, she said again in his mind.

Much to Edward's shock, he was even sorrier.

11

SAM SAT on the top of the blue bridge, watching the occasional car come along, wondering when a driver would look up and catch the idiot vampire just waiting to be found.

He was in a mood where the air was numb and everything seemed meaningless. Back at the house, Gisele was fighting for Edward, and Sam had lived much too long to miss the signs that everything had changed.

Sam, Gisele had said, mind-to-mind, before he'd left. *Please do not think you are being dismissed.*

But no matter how she said it or how many times he might come back, he knew this was how it would be now.

A car crept onto the bridge, and Sam had to stop himself from flagging it down, just to say, "Hey, I'm here! I still exist!"

But it wasn't the Dodge Aspen he'd been hoping for with every passing vehicle, only a green pickup with a faded paint job, bouncing along with a bale of hay in the bed.

The truck crossed the bridge in a fade of taillights, and Sam stood, lifting his face to the air, isolating the one scent that remained constant in all the disorder.

Corinna, and she wasn't very far.

Not far at all.

But if he went to her, he wouldn't be able to stop himself from biting her this time. And what if she screamed when she found out what he actually was? What if she cringed in fear and disgust as he expected every human to do?

Then again…

He thought of how, when Edward and Gisele were in the same room, the oxygen seemed to leave it. How there seemed to be nothing left for Sam to breathe.

He inhaled now, clearing his head.

Taking in Corinna.

Intoxicated, Sam shot away from the bridge, following her olfactory trail.

This is it, he thought. *No going back.*

The wind chopped against his face, his clothing, and it seemed as though only a heartbeat went by before he landed near the open window of a one-level brick house that sat away from a paved country lane. A few cars, including Corinna's Aspen, were in the long driveway, and he sensed other females living on the premises.

Relatives or roommates? he wondered, going to a window as the sheer yellow curtains belled away from the sill.

He peered inside, his sight cutting through the moon-tinted dimness to find a full-length antique mirror in a corner, framed pictures of night-slicked New Orleans streets, and a collection of sealed glass jars lined up on a vanity table and marked with labels such as Vanilla, Rosemary and Chamomile.

Sweet and fresh, he thought, also detecting a trace of incense. *Just like Corinna.*

When he came to the queen-sized bed with its sunny comforter, he grasped the windowsill, hardly believing what he saw.

She was already looking and smiling at him while re-clining against the pillows, dressed in a long pale night-dress, her arms wrapped around her bent legs. The grass bracelet remained around her wrist, intact.

How could she have known he was coming?

She answered in her typically endearing, fey way.

"I had a dream," she said quietly and without pream-ble. "Night after night, you were waiting by the bridge for me, but every time I came to meet you, you'd already left. Then *I* waited, but when I left, *you* came. Our timing was always off, and when I realized I'd never see you again, I finally woke up." Her smile grew wider. "But here you are, Sam, showing me I was just having a nightmare."

Her strange acceptance struck him. "You're still foggy from sleep."

"I've never been more awake."

He was itching to come inside, but she would have to invite him first. And once she did, he would have to face the truth that this wasn't just about a bite.

It was about finding what had been waiting for him all along.

"Where have you been?" she asked.

Should he tell her?

His pulse stuttered. What if she sent him off once she knew all the gory details? What would he do then?

"Sam, I don't get you." She frowned. "Here you are at my window, and it would all seem very romantic ex-cept for the one teeny fact that you've been gone the past few nights. After I laid that kiss on you, I've never seen a guy burn rubber like you did, and that ain't exactly a confidence builder."

Sam almost did a double take. If he'd suspected she

was sensitive before, he was certain now. She wasn't supposed to remember the part about him "burning rubber," not after he'd soothed her.

"You fell asleep before I left," he said, testing. "I'm not sure what you're—"

"You touched my head and then told me to sleep, and I started to, but I didn't quite get there."

They stared at each other. She knew something was off with him, but she wasn't screaming or carrying on.

Corinna waved him in. "Why don't you stay a while? But we'll have to keep our voices down. I've got two roommates who like their sleep, and since one of their parents owns this house, I don't particularly want to get kicked out. It's a nice place. A good deal for a girl who makes barely nine dollars an hour."

Furrowing his brow, he nonetheless climbed through the window, drawn to her mystery as well as just plain to *her*. Maybe he should've floated in, showing off what he could do, but he was still too skittish about how she might react to a revelation of his powers.

"So…" he said, not knowing where to start as he stood across the room.

"So. How about you tell me what was going on with that sleep thing? How did it almost knock me out like that?"

He paused, glancing around the room, as if it would give him an idea of how honest he should be.

But then he lit on some wooden bookshelves in a corner near the window—a spot he hadn't seen yet. Hardcovers and paperbacks, with titles such as *Tarot for Beginners* and *The World of Wicca* were piled willy-nilly.

Sam's eyes went wide as he flicked his gaze to the

glass jars on the vanity table. She had been looking for something special within her, he thought. But he hadn't suspected this was the direction she'd been searching.

Catching his perusal as well as his reaction, Corinna laughed softly.

"Did you put some kind of spell on me?" Sam asked.

"Oh, no. No, no, no. I'm just a dabbler who burns incense, really, and I've collected a few materials, just to make sachets, but I don't attempt spells."

"Not even to get your ex-boyfriend to come back to you? One of those things could've backfired and summoned a look-alike. That's where I'd come in."

"Sam." She motioned toward her shelves. "Check out more of the titles and you'll see religious studies and philosophy, too, even though I haven't even cracked those yet. They seemed real interesting in the store though. All of it's interesting."

He remembered that initial night, when he had sensed a person who liked to balance above the river, who peered into its dark spots but kept to the moonlight.

Corinna still hugged her knees. "So here I was trying to open my world when you came along. I suppose it kept me aware, so I knew there was something different about you from the very first second."

"I'm different, all right."

The way he said it made her glance at him sidelong.

Sam took a deep breath, then exhaled. Truth or bust—he couldn't stand another second of this. "I'm more like…not human at all."

Five heartbeats must have passed before she said, "Come again?"

Okay. Mistake. He should've told her he was a practicing warlock and left it at that.

By now she had unlocked her arms from around her legs, and even that little movement stirred the air with her delicious scent.

"Sam?" she asked, her voice smaller now.

"I'm a vampire."

He braced himself for her sharp intake of breath, her gurgling attempt at a screech that would bring her room-mates running.

But neither materialized.

Instead, she was smiling again. "Wow." Her smile grew even wider. *"Wow."* Now she hit the side of her head. "The cold skin. The mind trick. The speed when you zipped over to 'save' me on the bridge when we met. And, you know, your eyes are real vivid, but I just thought you maybe wore contacts or…"

She stopped talking. "A *vampire.*"

No fear. Only wonder.

If she'd been searching for some meaning these past few years, she'd stumbled on an unlikely twist, but he saw her embracing it, even from across the room.

"Are you going to scream now?" he asked. "Because sometimes it takes a few seconds to sink in before humans do that. At least, that's what I've heard."

"No." She shook her head, her curls bouncing as she got to her knees in excitement. "I just…Sam, before you bite me, can you tell me what it's like?"

"Before I…?" Instead of her asking him if *he* was for real, he was wondering about *her.* "How do you know I'm going to bite you? I haven't the other times."

Her smile crumbled. "Right. I mean, why should my track record change, even if you *are* a vampire?"

Genius, Sam, he thought. The last thing she needed was to be rejected again, especially after what had gone on with the boyfriend she thought she'd be spending the rest of her life with.

"Corinna, that didn't come out right," he said quickly. "Boy, if you could only know how I've been dying for you."

The smile built itself back up, shining into Sam, piercing his chest.

"Really?" she asked.

"Yeah, but… Well, it's complicated."

"Too complicated to explain?"

"Pretty much."

Corinna spread out her hands. "You can do mind tricks. Just use them to explain everything to me. Can't you?"

He'd been invited inside.

It was all the permission Sam needed to go as deeply as he'd always wanted to.

He engaged her gaze, and it was like the frayed end of a wire connecting with another and coming to sizzling life. Her flailing pulse became his.

He saw what she offered first: the lingering shame and questions about being left behind by the man who had promised to be her husband after he graduated from college, the memories of the parents who had died in a small-plane crash just after her high-school graduation, her appreciation of an aunt who had become a substitute parent.

But Sam took the burden of all this away from Corinna, honoring her memories while easing the pain of them.

He showed her it was okay to move on by sharing his own human life, then his exchange with Fegan, his adventures with the vampire gang, his time with Gisele.

When he got to Edward, he stopped, unable to endure it.

Sam slowly withdrew, and Corinna blinked, coming back to reality.

"And that's me," he said simply, refusing to go back into her mind to see what she was thinking now.

"It seems…" Searching for the right words, she used her hands to find them. Then she rested her hands in her lap. "It seems like being a vampire made all the difference for you."

"I wouldn't want to be any other way."

At least, that's how he'd always seen things. But without a gang, without Gisele, without anyone to explore the world with, he wasn't sure now.

"Sam," she added, her dark eyes wide, "you didn't show me what would happen if you bit me. I'm not talking about exchanging with me but…just a bite?"

At her reluctance to ask for the full blood exchange, Sam grew a little less animated. He wanted Corinna as a companion, but it was a huge decision for anyone. Still, because of what he'd felt for her, he'd hoped she would return the desire to be with him.

Maybe she didn't want that—didn't want *him* at all.

Seeming to understand his disappointment—even without a mind-link—she smiled. "Just a bite…for now?"

Did that mean there was a future?

He couldn't ask because his fangs emerged more quickly than usual.

Seeing the change come to him, she exhaled on an aroused shiver, then pushed her hair away from her neck. But she was smiling, too, as if she'd finally arrived at the last page of all the books she'd bought.

His vision throbbed, just as his body did.

"So you're clear," he said, his voice strangled, "a bite can bring out different things in different people."

"I'm ready to be brought out then. There's a reason we found each other, you realize that, Sam?"

Yes, he did, and it all made perfect sense now as he crawled onto her mattress, trying so hard to contain his anticipation.

Still, the *pound, pound* of his heartbeat made her expand and retract in his crimson sight.

Closer…closer.

As he drew up to her, he could see a vein in her neck pulsing, inviting. Her breath was coming quick and short, and when he reached out to touch her, she bit the inside of her lips, as if expecting pain.

It was time for some swaying, because the last thing Sam wanted to do was hurt her in any way.

He modulated his voice. "It's like a kiss, Corinna. Think of how much you wanted that the other night."

And she did think about it, her body relaxing as Sam got to his knees and took her in his arms, burying his face in her hair.

His pulse quickened. She smelled so good, like the only sustenance that would ever nourish him.

She rested the tips of her fingers against his chest, then crept them up his neck to his jaw. Then she canted her face to him, seeking his lips with hers.

When they kissed, a shock rattled them both, and their fingers dug into hair and skin. Her mouth was much softer than he recalled, possibly because he wasn't stressing out about what he was this time.

No, now this was true, right. The only present and future that existed.

They tasted each other, almost shyly exploring, the kiss becoming more demanding as they became more familiar.

She pressed her hand against the back of his head,

wanting more from their mouths, and when she slipped her tongue inside, he hesitated.

His fangs, he thought.

But she was curious, experimenting by touching one with the tip of her tongue, then running along his gums to try the other one.

Pulling away, she whispered, "Sharp. I'll need to be careful every time."

Every time.

Sam kissed his way to the tips of her mouth, over her jaw, to her neck, where her skin was tight and smooth. Where her vein beat at him like a summoning drum.

He whispered to her, stroking her throat, bringing her up and up to a place that would never hurt.

She was so responsive; many humans took a lot more attention until they were primed for a bite—sexually, mentally. But Corinna was already there.

"Now," she said, leading his face to her neck. "Now, Sam."

Willing to do anything for her, he rubbed his mouth over the intended spot—soft, enticing—and gently drove his fangs into her.

At the pop of the bite, she clutched at him, but he could feel that it wasn't in anguish—not the bad kind, anyway. She was already moaning and leaning back, falling to the bed. As he lowered her to the mattress, she wrapped a leg over the backs of his thighs, urging him closer, length to length.

Sam was hard, and he only got harder as he sucked, Corinna's hips grinding against him while she panted and gripped at his shirt.

Passion built—her blood throbbing, his mouth nursing. Every beat was a step forward, not back, never back again.

Their thoughts—deep red, thick and bold—entwined, so did their limbs, their fingers as they clasped hands and held to each other.

Another step forward, another…

Finally, with a final suck, a final thrust against her pantie-covered sex, they exploded together, two becoming one, vining through each other until neither of them had a beginning or end.

And in the spinning aftermath, as they unwound, he touched her neck, healing her in so many ways.

They looked into each other's eyes, and he knew that he wouldn't have to clear her mind of the bite. So instead of touching her temples, he brushed his fingers down her palm, over the grass bracelet that had bound them nights ago.

When she raised her trembling hand to look at it, the grass had become a temporary green, just like a renewed chance.

Laughing, Corinna used that hand to smooth back Sam's hair. "So what do you do for an encore?"

His smile grew melancholy as he leaned into his companion's palm.

Because an encore would have to include going back to his old home one more time to say goodbye.

AFTER ESCAPING Gisele, Edward had headed toward his stash in a cavern just outside Lexington. It was only one of the many places he had stored money and gold, his share of the loot from the old days with the gang. He'd also stored the few personal possessions he utilized to survive, including a change of clothing.

As the walls surrounded him, he had tried to tell himself that he shouldn't go back to Gisele's hideaway, that he should never see her again. He even shivered with the effort it took to keep him away, then dressed in the spare boots, shirt and long coat before flying into the night in the opposite direction.

Soon, he found a very willing female truck driver for sustenance, then swayed her and fed her human fast food from a twenty-four-hour drive-in so she would regain strength as she slept. Leaving her to wake on her own without recalling what had happened, he flew a short distance until the sun rose and forced him to an old shed on some neglected farm property that would shield him from the coming day.

He repeated much the same process the next night and the next, seeking sanctuary, heading toward a place that would allow him to piece his head together.

When he arrived at Stephen's isolated cabin in Big Bear, California, the moon was glistening on the nearby lake, and his old friend was working away at a computer in the downstairs study while his wife and child were abed upstairs.

Edward tapped on the window, using a code from the gang days.

Recognizing it immediately, Stephen turned around in his chair, then motioned toward the front porch where they always met. A tall, sturdy human now, Stephen had nevertheless kept his light-brown hair long, which gave him an artistic air in this day and age. His clothing—an untucked, roomy, white button-down and threadbare jeans—only added to it.

Edward was already sitting on the well-oiled porch swing, listening to the crickets and frogs, when Stephen shut the screen door behind him.

"Haven't seen you in a while," he said in a British

accent that had been filed away by the years spent in America. He leaned against the log wall. "You look as though you have been dragged up a mountain and then down again."

"I found Gisele."

Stephen dropped into a rough-hewn chair, his welcoming demeanor now serious. "You are still vampire, so I assume you didn't kill her."

"I…couldn't."

For the next hour, Edward told Stephen everything: the taming, the fighting, the utter confusion that debilitated him even now.

"I hate to venture this," Stephen said, "but I would guess that taming of yours was for the better."

Edward started to deny it. No use anymore. "Maybe Gisele's lessons were the capper to all the lectures you and the boys have been giving me," he said instead.

Out of nowhere, a female voice interrupted from behind the screen door. "It sounds to me as if, instead of a soul, you found a soulmate."

The door opened, and a pale-skinned redhead came out dressed in a nightgown and robe, her long hair sleep-ruffled. She'd been eavesdropping.

"Good to see you, Edward," Kimberly, Stephen's wife, said.

"Hello, Kimberly. Sorry to have woken you." Edward's mouth was moving, but his mind was still catching up to the truth of what she had said.

A soulmate. Gisele.

While looking for one thing, he'd found what he actually needed.

Kimberly had shrugged at his apology. "We don't get

vampires visiting every night. Just ex-bloodsuckers, but that's not half as exciting to us humans."

She had a way of talking bravely, just as she had done when Edward had threatened her life when he was the rogue. Although they had come to terms with that, neither of them would ever forget.

"Edward," she said, pursuing the story, as was another habit of hers. "From the way you told your tale, it sounds as if you wouldn't mind going back to her." She glanced down at her husband. "A girl can sniff that sort of thing out, you know."

"Yes, especially this girl." Stephen pulled her down to his lap. "Listening in, were you?"

Kimberly nodded, then aimed an expectant gaze at Edward.

But he was too busy dwelling on Kimberly's observation.

…wouldn't mind going back to her.

But how could he do that?

Edward held his pulse steady. It wasn't easy looking at Kimberly, knowing that he'd once threatened her. She'd forgiven him, but he'd never believed it possible.

"Gisele is just as sorry as I am," he said.

Kimberly reared back. "You *do* sound tamed. Is this the Edward we all know or are you a doppelgänger? And that's a real question."

"I am…" Edward searched for something, anything, but came up empty. "I don't know what I am anymore."

Kimberly stood. "Tea. I think you old Brits need tea out here."

She went back inside, leaving the males alone.

They sat in silence for a few moments, then Stephen leaned forward, his hands collapsed in front of him.

"Edward, the boys and I have said that humanity is not earned through the taking of it. Killing Gisele would have defeated the very purpose of what you wanted so badly. You grew past that. Shouldn't that be a comfort to you?"

"It should."

The human held up a dismissive hand then lowered it, shaking his head. "You have always needed something to blame for life's woes. But now that you have stumbled upon the precipice of happiness, you back away."

Edward huffed and gazed at the lake, shards of moonlight stabbing its surface. "Happiness? Put me and Gisele in the same room, and it's murder."

"Oh, is that why you're here? Because she killed you and you killed her?"

None of it made sense, but then again, it made all the sense in the world.

"She can't want to be with me," Edward said.

Stephen stood, going toward the screen door. "Believe it or not, Gisele is capable of affection. It's only that you think you don't deserve it."

Edward got out of his seat, too. "And that would solve everything? Admitting I deserve it."

"It would be a start. You have come a long way in vanquishing all that hatred, Edward, and I'm relieved to see it. But, you stubborn fool, you need to work this out with her. She is your answer to what we all search for in life and existence, and you can seize that and finally experience the greatest gift this earth holds, or you can be a brooding shadow that wastes the rest of his nights wondering what might have happened. It's your choice, but it is not going to be resolved a continent away from where you clearly would rather be."

With that, Stephen stepped across his threshold, then held the door open for his guest.

But Edward stood still.

He kept remembering how decimated Gisele had been when he'd left. And maybe, just maybe, he'd even carried through with his escape because he'd *known* it would hurt her.

He was tired of inflicting damage. Tired of running. Tired of battling what every cell of his body demanded.

Stephen's voice came through in a mist. "Coming inside, old man?"

"Not tonight," Edward said, rising into the air and taking wing east.

Back toward the hideaway.

Back toward his last chance at finding the answers for which he'd always been searching.

12

THE WIND howled through the maple tree as Gisele sat in the cradle of its branches, peeking through the leaves and into the window of a house.

She was at Terrence Gorley's three-story pseudo-mansion, and she could see into his state-of-the-art family entertainment room with its fully stocked bar, Ping-Pong table and wide-screen television.

Presently, her neighbor was sitting on a couch in front of the TV, his arm around a brunette he had asked out for the very first time.

Gisele's bite had given him this confidence, and the female was responding to his ramped-up sexual pull with coy interest. She kept inching closer, reaching for the popcorn bowl on his lap, laughing at the jokes he was telling while they watched a classic-movie station broadcasting the black-and-white splendor of Kurosawa's *The Hidden Fortress*.

It was not that Gisele was there to spy or to feed in some way off their growing intimacy. She was watching the movie, just as she used to as a human.

But, moment by moment, she grew more uncomfortable with this viewing, because the more enthralled the woman became, the more Gisele was reminded of the last time she had been in a theater.

She drifted down from the tree and back to the hide-away, not knowing what should come next.

No Edward. No Sam.

Both had been away for nights, but she had expected that. She was only surprised Sam had not come by to say farewell, since she had been using their mental connection to reach out to wherever he was and show him what had happened with Edward.

Edward...

A severe pain wracked her as she entered her empty house. Perhaps she would pack now, leave this place where she saw all the missteps she had made. She had only stayed here in the hope that someone would return.

But no one ever did.

Resigned, she gathered what meager belongings she required, doing her best to ignore her surroundings, the items filled with overwhelming significance.

The bed in the attic she had made for Edward.

The clothing she had worn to tempt him.

The chains that were still on the family-room floor, shed just as rightfully as she had been.

She sank to the floor near the chains, closing her eyes, and decided to rest here for just one more day.

Just in case someone did return....

When the sun lowered again, she awoke, then thought that perhaps she should feed before she decided what else to do. But she was lacking the will to hunt.

What had she told Edward all those nights ago? That not feeding would make for a withered, helpless creature?

But what if she had already become one?

She sat at the kitchen table, telling herself to move. Telling herself that the silent parade of future nights would be bearable if she could just get out of the chair and occupy herself, thus allowing the hours to pass without dragging.

But then...

Then she felt a nuzzling against her senses and, at first, she thought it was Edward. Her heart seemed to open wide, bursting with happiness.

I knew it, she thought. *He did not want to leave.*

Then her senses retuned themselves, latching on to the feel of a friend who had come home instead.

Her heart dropped, but filled again with a different sort of joy. She sprinted to the window, pushing aside the covering, knowing who it was now.

Sam stood on a hill in the backyard, near the barn, his hands in his pockets. The girl, Corinna, was slightly behind him, looking just as she had in Sam's adoring flashbacks except for a glow that had not been there before; she had obviously been bitten.

Gisele opened the back screen door, waiting at the threshold, hoping Sam was here to stay because it might ease the agony of having Edward gone.

Yet as soon as she thought it, she knew it was not fair to Sam. Not fair at all.

She walked outside, past where the tent used to be, then up the incline.

Sam had turned to Corinna, looking so deeply into her eyes that Gisele paused, fixing her gaze instead on the weatherbeaten barn, a few missing slats leaving gaps in the facade. Through them, she could scent old hay, sweet yet musty. She could also see a rope that was connected to the loft, and she imagined wrapping it around her own wrists in an attempt to redeem what she had done to Edward.

Sam had walked to Gisele by now, and when she

glanced at him, she saw that Corinna had remained behind, gazing after him.

They were silent at first, because there was nothing quite right to say.

Finally, she whispered, "You have not turned her."

"Not yet." Sam was searching Gisele's face, probably refusing to touch minds, probably because it now seemed out of line. "I've only been showing her what would be in store if she ever decides to exchange."

"She does not want it?"

"It's actually more that I don't want her to make a rash decision. Still, she's been ready for it a long, long time—way before I even got here."

"But you learned from my errors." Gisele's throat burned. "That's my smart Sam."

"Yeah."

She bit down on her lip, realizing he was acknowledging more that he *used* to be her Sam than anything.

He kicked at the overgrown grass, and she knew that this was just as rough for him as it was for her.

"We've been talking a lot about what happens next," he said.

Gisele nodded, her throat closed now.

"She's always wanted to travel," he added. "Mainly to places that have an otherworldly vibe about them. We're thinking of heading to Charleston first, after Corinna says goodbye to her aunt and friends."

"Charleston is sufficiently haunted."

"Isn't everything?"

A beat passed, and Sam reached out to take her in his arms. She accepted the embrace, tears coming to her eyes; she gave in to them only because of Sam's goodbye.

Or perhaps because of Edward, too.

"We can stay," her former partner said, no doubt reacting to her tears. "I picked up on your mental signals, so I knew you were okay after the final confrontation with Edward, but I thought you might need some time to pull yourself together. You never did like to show weakness in front of me, just like any good creator."

She wiped at her eyes, wishing the tears would stop, even if they felt as if they had needed to come for so long now. "You wish to stay because I am blubbering?"

Inhaling a deep breath, she knew what had to come next, even though she did not want to add yet another loss to her growing list.

But it was time for Sam to go.

She pulled away from him. "You will be her creator now."

"How about that," he said. "A creator."

A cleansing laugh cut through her tears. Her Sam. Not her Sam now.

"You knew everything would be right the first instant you found someone who gives even the smallest of details meaning," she said. "Have you told her you love her?"

"I've been working up to that, too, even though I think she knows."

Gisele rested her fingertips against his cheek, memorizing him in case she never saw him again. "Whatever you do, do not fight it."

Cupping his hand over hers, Sam gazed at her. "Do you want to come with *us* then?"

"We both know it is not a good idea."

"Then what are you going to do?"

She squeezed his fingers. "I will find something."

"Maybe there'll be another you'll connect to, or—"

"No, there will not be any others."

Sam seemed to grow worried about her, his forehead creasing. "And if Edward comes back?"

"If," she said.

"I think he will, Gisele. From what you showed me in your mind, he'll return someday, and it won't be to harm you."

"Sam—"

"Don't 'Sam' me. You love him and he came to feel the same way about you, and it's driving both of you nuts because you have no idea how to handle it. You told me that I knew Corinna was my true companion the first time I laid eyes on her and, basically, it'll just take a little longer for you and Edward to admit the same thing." Sam took a breath to make up for the diatribe. "Will you track him down this time?"

"No." Because that was the reality. Companions left, so did parents and creators. Everyone did.

She got ready to say goodbye to yet another.

"Don't you dare worry about me, Sam Collins," Gisele said, giving him a graceful way to exit.

In spite of her sorrow, she patted his cheeks, and he got that perpetually twentyish aw-shucks expression so exclusive to American boys who grew up long before beings like her realized it.

"Go to her," she said.

As if tempted beyond measure, Sam glanced over his shoulder to where Corinna was waiting. She raised a tentative hand, and he stepped back from Gisele.

It felt as if he were already a million miles away.

He impulsively took her into one last hug, and they clung to each other, recalling what they used to have before parting.

"Go," Gisele said lightly, waving him away and suppressing more tears.

He went, looking back at her before taking to his heels and speeding over to Corinna, who already had her arms open. When he got to her, he swept her into an embrace, swinging her around. And when he set her down, he spoke into her ear so softly that Gisele could not even hear.

But she knew what he was saying.

I love you....

Which Corinna said back to him, out loud and exuberantly.

The couple held hands, and Gisele's gaze linked with Corinna's, passing on the torch to a companion who would treasure Sam in all the ways he deserved.

A blast of heat singed both her head and chest, but she thought it was because she was slowly ashing apart, never to be brought together again.

Then Sam was glancing at something behind Gisele and, at first, she could not identify what was happening.

There was only electricity, heat.

She turned around, consumed, already knowing....

And there stood Edward inside the barn, near the rope. He was dark, sexy and dressed much as he had been the first night, in his rough canvas pants and another long coat.

An assassin who was here to see to the last of her?

No. Because she saw that look in his eyes again—the longing, the deep desire, the...affection?

Gisele went liquid, and she knew that her eyes told him the same.

Should I stay? she heard Sam say via their minds.

Without hesitation, she shook her head, then answered, *You were right. He is not here to kill me.*

Sam paused as he gauged Edward, as well. Then his mind-voice went soft. *It really is time for me to leave then.*

She took one last glance at her old companion and his new one.

Sam. Corinna's Sam.

With a lift of his hand, he waved one last goodbye, then turned around with Corinna, withdrawing in a wisp of sharp absence.

Then she began walking toward Edward, holding her breath and hoping she was not wrong about why he had returned.

"I'M NOT here to kill you," he said as soon as Gisele walked into the barn, past the old, scattered bales of hay and agonizingly close to him.

He wanted to reach out to her, but he feared that she might misconstrue an action that had often been aggressive between them.

Could they really overcome everything?

Edward had to try, because he didn't want to become one of those revenants he had mentioned to Sam before—beings cursed to an unfeeling existence—when there was so much for him to finally open himself to.

So much that Gisele had introduced him to.

She had stopped a few feet in front of him, and her body heat filled his senses, the blood racing under her skin, the thud of her heartbeat overcoming him.

"I visited Stephen and Kimberly," he added, taking his own first step toward her, lured, helpless around her. But he knew this was more than sex. This was about two beings who had experienced the sensation of being one, and it was all but impossible to tear away from someone who understood the depths of his darkness and still wanted to shed light on them.

"I am glad to know you were safe," she said, as if testing where this would lead.

But she also said it with such sincerity that his pulse doubled in time.

"I didn't find all the answers there," he added, "and who knows if I ever will, but I did come away knowing this: I'm not certain how to exist with you, but I know it would be impossible to do it without you."

Tilting her head, she reached out slowly and took hold of his coat. An attachment that didn't include chains.

It was a start.

"When I apologized to you for losing control with that bite," she said, "I meant so much more than just that. I am sorry for everything, then and now."

He had already come to terms with that last bite, and it helped him to see he could also accept everything about her…and himself. Leaving her—leaving the chance for redemption that she had offered both of them—had been a fool's choice. She'd been the only one who had ever made him believe a new beginning was possible.

They could both start over again.

Yet how would they get beyond this point?

She was clearly thinking the same, trying to find neutral ground between them. "Sam left."

"It was high time for him to strike out on his own. What surprises me is that you let him go."

"It…surprised me, too."

She reached out for the rope that dangled next to him, then glanced at him as she ran her hand down its length.

"I keep thinking," she said, "that I was so avid about taming you when I needed it in so many ways myself."

Would they ever move past the taming, the hurt, the lack of trust?

He sauntered toward the rope, too, and her lips parted. Those luscious red lips that had given him too much pleasure to ever forget. He went soft…and hard.

So very hard.

She handed the rope to him.

His brain searched for the meaning of her gesture, even though he already knew.

"You wish for me to…tame you," he said.

"To make us equal," she said, and he could feel that this was not only a symbolic gesture, but the very idea was escalating her pulse, making her skin give off waves of desire.

"Gisele," he whispered.

Slowly, she reached out to run her fingers down his cheekbones, his jaw, her eyes filled with an affection that shook him.

Then she held up her other hand, offering both wrists to him.

Carefully, he wrapped the rope around them.

Her pulse kicked up to another level, and as she left her mind open for him, he could see that she had gone a bit dark, her memories flickering.

She didn't articulate it, but she was wondering if he would leave when she was at her most helpless.

That's what this was really about, he thought. And he could prove himself to her and him; he could build the first block of trust for the foundation they would need.

It was one step that would get them to the next point.

"Trust me," he said. "I came back, and I'm not going anywhere now. I don't want to."

When she gave him a look filled with heartbreaking

doubt—she still didn't believe him—he reached out to her mind, caressing it.

And when she opened more to him, he sent a burst of warmth into her.

She gasped, leaning back her head, her body trembling as he suffused her. He even felt as if something were being pulled out of him and into her, like a beam binding them.

He took her pain and she took his, and the sharing of it eased both of them.

At that moment, the reason that their scents were so engrained in each other, their pheromones attuned to a perfect chemistry—the reason they had been fated to be together—shone over everything.

He could help her rise above the past, too.

On a surprised sound that was half laugh, half moan, she sank to her knees, her arms extended over her head, her eyes wide and full of wonder at what had just happened.

"More, Edward."

Her voice had lowered, and it made him go red as he took in his kneeling companion, her body slim in the sleeveless beige sheath she wore, her arms still bound.

It was an echo of his own taming, when she had driven him wild while he'd been restrained, dying to reach out to her.

She eased her mind into his now. *Touch me. Come into me again.*

He got to one knee, trailing his fingers over her lips. Then, testing her, he raised both of his hands up to her wrists, skimming down her arms until she squirmed at the ticklish contact, bucking toward him.

Her sex contracted—with their solidified bond, he could feel it in his cock.

Gasping, they stared at each other. Previously, they had only shared orgasms.

"Oh, what a time we are going to have after all," she said.

A wicked grin broke out on his lips as he traced his fingers over her breasts, the tips pebbling with the first pass. His own skin tingled, too.

"Edward," she groaned.

With one yank, he ripped at her neckline, splitting the dress and exposing her pale body. At the mere sight of her deep-red nipples, the nest of hair between her legs, he was primed to bite.

He bent very low, pressing her hips forward so he could lick her sex. Then he continued upward, smoothing his tongue over her belly, over her stomach, between her breasts, over her neck. Her scent invaded, tangling him up in knots.

At the same time, he felt as if a line of fire had divided his body, and his head ticked, his cock throbbed. He and Gisele had been ready for each other for so long.

He rubbed his face against her neck, her hair soft against his skin, and as she strained at her rope to get to him, he lifted his face to capture her lips with his.

It was as if the ticking in his head had only been a countdown. As they kissed each other, their fangs cut, their mouths devoured. Their blood mixed and they sipped it from each other, greedy for everything they could exchange.

Gisele churned her hips against his erection, and he released himself from his trousers, guiding his penis to her and pushing a palm against one of her legs to open her further.

As his cock probed her drenched sex, both of them reared back from their kiss, as they sought breath.

Then, with a sure thrust, he entered her, and they both cried out, her using the rope as leverage as he drove into her again and again.

"I want…" he said, "…all of you."

"But—" She grunted with another thrust. "—a bite?"

It had driven him away last time, but not now.

He led her toward his neck, still pummeling, pummeling into her, and she simultaneously guided him toward her throat, too.

Equals, they thought together. Redemption in one another.

They reared back, then plunged their fangs into each other at the same time, and he kept hammering into her, their sucks echoing the rhythm. It was a new exchange, erasing the old, creating them all over again as they literally rose from the ground to hover above it.

All but weightless, they floated, mingled, became one being.

One existence.

With a raging rush, they peaked, hitting the roof of the barn, then began falling…

The rope snapped and they crashed to the ground, the breath jarred out of them. They kept holding on to each other, panting, bodies warmed and blazing, like suns melding into a bigger power.

"I could learn to love this," Edward said against Gisele's neck as his fangs receded.

Hers did the same as she whispered, "Just as I could learn to love you."

He tightened his arms around her, breathing easily now that he had found what he had always been missing.

"I have already learned."

Spent and satiated, their heartbeats evened out, trading punches against each other's chests as they lay, bound together.

Epilogue

GISELE WAS hungry tonight.

But she knew just what she needed now, five months after Edward had come back to her.

From across the ornate lobby of the Hotel Monteleone in the revitalized French Quarter, he caught her adoring gaze and grinned. It was a promise that she would indeed be well fed after they took care of business.

When she spotted their "student" striding his own way into the room, she went on alert. It did not do to call them "marks" anymore, seeing as the hunt had an entirely different purpose now.

He was a balding, skinny CEO of a mortgage company, dressed in a tuxedo for the party he would be attending in a Garden District mansion. Research had told them that Daniels and his associates were taking advantage of Katrina victims: after promising to defer loans, the company had gone back on their word, forcing clients to pay their monthly installments immediately or face losing their homes.

As the human headed for the door, Gisele intercepted him. He slowed his steps, no doubt because of the care she had taken to look good in a long, flaring white dress that did all it could for her cleavage.

"Excuse me?" she asked, resurrecting her French inflection…and the sway of her voice.

"A girl like you doesn't have to be excused," he said smoothly, coming to a stop, already reeled in.

Behind him, she could see Edward making his way through the crowd and toward the exit where they would whisk Mr. Daniels, followed by five of his friends, into a limousine and to a dark, waiting courtyard just outside of the Quarter.

As Edward passed, she did her best not to drop everything and follow him. She would save her enthusiasm for later.

She began to walk outside and Mr. Daniels, of course, followed.

"I wonder if you might show me where Irene's Cuisine is?" she asked, motioning toward the waiting limo.

He did not even have to be persuaded, even though he could have—*should* have—merely given her directions instead of coming along for the ride he was clearly expecting.

But she had him, just as he had "had" so many destitute mortals.

Smiling seductively, she got in to the darkness of the vehicle and guided him in with her.

Then she pushed him into the seat across from her. His eyes were already hazy from sexual expectation, and she seized the moment to flit her fingers over his temple.

"Sleep."

Mr. Daniels slumped against the seat and, from a spot next to him in the limo's dark corner, Edward spoke.

"Efficient, as always."

Gisele could not wait any longer.

She leaned across the space to kiss her companion,

and Edward responded with equal fervor before they came back up for air.

Then, with a commanding tug, he pulled her all the way onto his lap. "Now we go to intercept his friends."

"We will provide a better party than the one they were going to anyway."

Since she knew Edward would always feel guilty about feeding from mortals, she had suggested a way for them to address that. They hunted human predators, and after Gisele fed from the willing men, Edward would feed off her. Then, of course, came the most important part: when they "persuaded" the students to turn their lives around.

They were even on her own creator's trail, determined to do the same with him, if possible. Edward was adamant about seeing to it.

Her dark knight, she thought, smoothing back his long hair. He was fulfilling his vampiric potential, partnering with her in balancing the scales.

"Hey back there," said a male voice through the half-lowered glass partition. "Is this really the time for getting fresh?"

From the driver's seat, Sam glanced in the rear view mirror, his eyes twinkling. Next to him, Corinna laughed and slid the partition open all the way.

"I never get enough of these kinds of scumbags," she said. "But they're definitely not the best mankind has to offer—in blood or ethics."

Sam sighed. "That's the thing with new vampires. Always thinking of a meal."

Corinna gave him a slight push, and they smiled. He had turned her four months ago, before they had met up with Edward and Gisele in New Orleans. It worked well this way—seeing each other every so often, then having couple time.

Edward nuzzled Gisele's neck. She kissed his forehead, so thankful for how far they had all come.

As they kept driving onward, their fingers twined, connecting, never to separate through all the nights they had yet to spend together.

* * * * *

Here's a sneak peek at
THE CEO'S CHRISTMAS PROPOSITION,
the first in USA TODAY *bestselling author*
Merline Lovelace's HOLIDAYS ABROAD *trilogy*
coming in November 2008.

American Devon McShay is about to get the
Christmas surprise of a lifetime when she meets
her new client, sexy billionaire Caleb Logan, for
the very first time.

Silhouette
Desire

Available November 2008

Her breath whistled out in a sigh of relief when he exited Customs. Devon recognized him right away from the newspaper and magazine articles her friend and partner Sabrina had looked up during her frantic prep work.

Caleb John Logan, Jr. Thirty-one. Six-two. With jet-black hair, laser-blue eyes and a linebacker's shoulders under his charcoal-gray cashmere overcoat. His jaw-dropping good looks didn't score him any points with Devon. She'd learned the hard way not to trust handsome heartbreakers like Cal Logan.

But he was a client. An important one. And she was willing to give someone who'd served a hitch in the marines before earning a B.S. from the University of Oregon, an MBA from Stanford and his first million at the ripe old age of twenty-six the benefit of the doubt.

Right up until he spotted the hot-pink pashmina, that is.

Devon knew the flash of color was more visible than the sign she held up with his name on it. So she wasn't surprised when Logan picked her out of the crowd and cut in her direction. She'd just plastered on her best businesswoman smile when he whipped an arm around her waist. The next moment she was sprawled against his cashmere-covered chest.

"Hello, brown eyes."

Swooping down, he covered her mouth with his.

Sheer astonishment kept Devon rooted to the spot for a few seconds while her mind whirled chaotically. Her first thought was that her client had downed a few too many drinks during the long flight. Her second, that he'd mistaken the kind of escort and consulting services her company provided. Her third shoved everything else out of her head.

The man could kiss!

His mouth moved over hers with a skill that ignited sparks at a half dozen flash points throughout her body. Devon hadn't experienced that kind of spontaneous combustion in a while. A *long* while.

The sparks were still popping when she pushed off his chest, only now they fueled a flush of anger.

"Do you always greet women you don't know with a lip-lock, Mr. Logan?"

A smile crinkled the skin at the corners of his eyes. "As a matter of fact, I don't. That was from Don."

"Huh?"

"He said he owed you one from New Year's Eve two years ago and made me promise to deliver it."

She stared up at him in total incomprehension. Logan hooked a brow and attempted to prompt a non-existent memory.

"He abandoned you at the Waldorf. Five minutes before midnight. To deliver twins."

"I don't have a clue who or what you're…"

Understanding burst like a water balloon.

"Wait a sec. Are you talking about Sabrina's old boy-friend? Your buddy, who's now an ob-gyn doc?"

It was Logan's turn to look startled. He recovered

faster than Devon had, though. His smile widened into a rueful grin.

"I take it you're not Sabrina Russo."

"No, Mr. Logan, I am *not.*"

* * * * *

Be sure to look for
THE CEO'S CHRISTMAS PROPOSITION
by Merline Lovelace.
Available in November 2008 wherever books are sold, including most bookstores, supermarkets, drugstores and discount stores.

MARRIED BY CHRISTMAS

Playboy billionaire Elijah Vanaldi has discovered he is guardian to his small orphaned nephew. But his reputation makes some people question his ability to be a father. He knows he must fight to protect the child, and he'll do anything it takes. Ainslie Farrell is jobless, homeless and desperate—and when Elijah offers her a position in his household she simply can't refuse....

Available in November

HIRED: THE ITALIAN'S CONVENIENT MISTRESS
by
CAROL MARINELLI

Book #29

HPE82375

REQUEST YOUR FREE BOOKS!

2 FREE NOVELS PLUS 2 FREE GIFTS!

Red-hot reads!

YES! Please send me 2 FREE Harlequin® Blaze™ novels and my 2 FREE gifts (gifts are worth about $10). After receiving them, if I don't wish to receive any more books, I can return the shipping statement marked "cancel". If I don't cancel, I will receive 6 brand-new novels every month and be billed just $4.24 per book in the U.S. or $4.71 per book in Canada, plus 25¢ shipping and handling per book and applicable taxes, if any*. That's a savings of 15% or more off the cover price! I understand that accepting the 2 free books and gifts places me under no obligation to buy anything. I can always return a shipment and cancel at any time. Even if I never buy another book, the two free books and gifts are mine to keep forever.

151 HDN ERVA   351 HDN ERUX

Name	(PLEASE PRINT)

Address	Apt. #

City	State/Prov.	Zip/Postal Code

Signature (if under 18, a parent or guardian must sign)

Mail to the **Harlequin Reader Service:**
IN U.S.A.: P.O. Box 1867, Buffalo, NY 14240-1867
IN CANADA: P.O. Box 609, Fort Erie, Ontario L2A 5X3

Not valid to current subscribers of Harlequin Blaze books.

Want to try two free books from another line?
Call 1-800-873-8635 or visit www.morefreebooks.com.

* Terms and prices subject to change without notice. N.Y. residents add applicable sales tax. Canadian residents will be charged applicable provincial taxes and GST. Offer not valid in Quebec. This offer is limited to one order per household. All orders subject to approval. Credit or debit balances in a customer's account(s) may be offset by any other outstanding balance owed by or to the customer. Please allow 4 to 6 weeks for delivery. Offer available while quantities last.

Your Privacy: Harlequin Books is committed to protecting your privacy. Our Privacy Policy is available online at www.eHarlequin.com or upon request from the Reader Service. From time to time we make our lists of customers available to reputable third parties who may have a product or service of interest to you. If you would prefer we not share your name and address, please check here. ☐

HB08R

HARLEQUIN®

Blaze™

COMING NEXT MONTH

#429 KISS & TELL Alison Kent
In the world of celebrity tabloids, Caleb MacGregor is the best. Once he smells a scandal, he makes sure the world knows. And that's exactly what Miranda Kelly is afraid of. Hiding behind her stage name, Miranda hopes she'll avoid his notice. And she does—until she invites Caleb into her bed.

#430 UNLEASHED Lori Borrill
It's a wild ride in more ways than one when Jessica Beane is corralled into a road trip by homicide detective Rick Marshall. Crucial evidence is missing and Jess is the key to unlocking not just the case, but their pent-up passion, as well!

#431 A BODY TO DIE FOR Kimberly Raye
Love at First Bite, Bk. 3
Vampire Viviana Darland is in Skull Creek, Texas, looking for one thing—an orgasm. Or more specifically, the only man who's ever given her one, vampire Garret Sawyer. She knows her end is near, and wants one good climax before she goes. And she intends to get it—before Garret delivers on his promise to kill her....

#432 HER SEXIEST SURPRISE Dawn Atkins
He's the best birthday gift ever! When Chloe Baxter makes a sexy wish on her birthday candles, she never expects Riley Connelly—her secret crush—to appear. Nor does she expect him to give her the hottest night of her life. It's so hot, why share just one night?

#433 RECKLESS Tori Carrington
Indecent Proposals, Bk. 1
Heidi Joblowski isn't a woman to leave her life to chance. Her plan? To marry her perfect boyfriend, Jesse, and have several perfect children. Unfortunately, the only perfect thing in her life lately is the sex she's been having with Jesse's best friend Kyle....

#434 IN A BIND Stephanie Bond
Sex for Beginners, Bk. 2
Flight attendant Zoe Smythe is working her last shift, planning her wedding... and doing her best to ignore the sexual chemistry between her and a seriously sexy Australian passenger. But when she reads a letter she'd written in college, reminding her of her most private, erotic fantasies...all bets are off!

www.eHarlequin.com

HBCNM1008BPA